the Cheetah girls

the Cheetah girls

In the House with Mouse!

Deborah Gregory

JUMP AT THE SUN

HYPERION PAPERBACKS FOR CHILDREN

NEW YORK

Fashion credits: Photography by Charlie Pizzarello.
Models: Davida Williams, Sabrina Millen, Sonya
Millen, Imani Parks, and Brandi Stewart. Apparel by:
Betsey Johnson, Daang Goodman for Tripp, NYC,
P. Fields and Nicole Miller. Hair by Julie McIntosh.
Makeup by Kathleen Herch and Tasha Vila. Fashion
styling by Nole Martin.

Printed in the United States of America
First Edition
1 3 5 7 9 10 8 6 4 2
This book is set in 12-point Palatino.
ISBN 0-7868-1478-0
Library of Congress Catalog Card Number: 00-108934
Visit www.cheetahgirls.com

For my old school girlene, Beverly Johnson—
Pay homage to the one who paved the way
for all the chocolate bronzinas today
with her supa-dupa sashay
on the runway to plenty payday.
You worked it, Supermodel!

The Cheetah Girls Credo

To earn my spots and rightful place in the world, I solemnly swear to honor and uphold the Cheetah Girls oath:

🐾 Cheetah Girls don't litter, they glitter. I will help my family, friends, and other Cheetah Girls whenever they need my love, support, or a *really* big hug.

🐾 All Cheetah Girls are created equal, but we are not alike. We come in different sizes, shapes, and colors, and hail from different cultures. I will not judge others by the color of their spots, but by their character.

- A true Cheetah Girl doesn't spend more time doing her hair than her homework. Hair extensions may be career extensions, but talent and skills will pay my bills.

- True Cheetah Girls *can* achieve without a weave—or a wiggle, jiggle, or a giggle. I promise to rely (mostly) on my brains, heart, and courage to reach my cheetah-licious potential!

- A brave Cheetah Girl isn't afraid to admit when she's scared. I promise to get on my knees and summon the growl power of the Cheetah Girls who came before me—including my mom, grandmoms, and the Supremes—and ask them to help me be strong.

- All Cheetah Girls make mistakes. I promise to admit when I'm wrong and will work to make it right. I'll also say I'm sorry, even when I don't want to.

- Grown-ups are not always right, but they are bigger, older, and louder. I will treat my teachers, parents, and people of authority with respect—and expect them to do the same!

- True Cheetah Girls don't run with wolves or hang with hyenas. True Cheetahs pick much better friends. I will not try to get other people's approval by acting like a copycat.

- To become the Cheetah Girl that only *I* can be, I promise not to follow anyone else's dreams but my own. No matter how much I quiver, shake, shiver, and quake!

- Cheetah Girls were born for adventure. I promise to learn a language other than my own and travel around the world to meet my fellow Cheetah Girls.

the cheetah girls

Chapter 1

We cannot believe how big Madison Square Garden is—a whole lot bigger than the Astrodome back home. It feels like everybody in New York is sitting right here with us at the Mariah Carey concert!

That's right, the Cheetah Girls are waiting for the "Butterfly" diva to come onstage and sing up a storm—along with about 70,000 other people who are packed into the arena, screaming at the top of their lungs, "Mariah, Mariah, Mariah!"

My twin sister, Angie, puts her hands over her ears because this is more noise than we're used to, but I'm having too much fun to mind. See, we usually feel the same way about things, because we're identical twins in every way. The only way you can tell us apart is that Angie has a beauty mark on her left cheek.

The rest of the Cheetah Girls don't mind the noise or big crowds, because they grew up in New York City and are used to its hectic, rowdy ways.

The Cheetah Girls, of course, are: Galleria "Bubbles" Garibaldi, Chanel "Miss Cuchifrita" Simmons (she got her new nickname because of her latest ballet capers, which have landed her on crutches, thank you, ma'am!), Dorinda "Do' Re Mi" Rogers, and, of course, your favorite singing twins from Houston—little ol' me, Aquanette Walker, and my other half, Anginette. (Obviously, it's no secret which one has the bigger mouth, and tends to hog all the attention. Angie is quieter than I am—and sneakier, too!)

We still cannot believe how we got to be sitting in these too-small-for-our-butts seats tonight. It's all because Dorinda got twenty-five free tickets. (Yes, ma'am, from our mouths to God's ears!) Actually, Dorinda got to be *in charge* of the twenty-five tickets, because they were given to her foster mother, Mrs. Bosco.

In the House with Mouse!

What happened was, the foster care agency contacted Mrs. Bosco to take in an abandoned toddler named Gaye who was left by her little self to wander around the Coney Island projects. The police department tried really hard to find Gaye's family—they put up big posters all over the city and everything. Even the local TV news stations ran stories showing her picture, but nobody came forward with any information. (New York is sooo big, you cannot imagine all the people who live here and don't even know each other's business, like they do back home.) Anyway, even though Mrs. Bosco already had eleven mouths to feed, she took Gaye in all the same.

I look over at Gaye, who has the cutest little dimples and the biggest, saddest brown eyes. She's sitting very still in her seat, with her hands folded in her lap and her legs dangling back and forth.

"I'll bet she must be around four years old," I whisper in Angie's ear, even though she can't hear me—but she figures it out when I flash four fingers under her nose. (Twins can read each other's minds, too.)

It's still hard to believe that a mother would

do something as evil as abandoning her child. But Big Momma, our grandmother back home in Houston, says, "Sometimes people lose their way, then lose their minds." We put Gaye in our prayers now, and we're never gonna take *our* parents for granted again—even if they are dee-vorced. And even though Daddy is acting stranger than ever—which I'll tell you more about in a minute.

But first, I know you must be wondering what any of this has to do with Mariah Carey. Well, when Mariah heard about Gaye on the news, she was so touched by the story that she had her record company contact the foster care agency, and provide free tickets to her concert for Mrs. Bosco and all her foster kids. There were more than enough tickets to go around— which is how the Cheetah Girls came to be here, too.

It's funny how things work out. For Thanksgiving, Angie and I pulled a few strings to get the rest of the Cheetah Girls to come down to Houston and spend Thanksgiving with our family—*and* to perform with us in the "Houston Helps Its Own" charity concert. (Yes, ma'am, the concert folks actually paid for the rest of the Cheetah Girls to fly down!) Now, Dorinda has pulled *her* strings to make sure we're here with her and her family—taking up twenty-five seats in a row. One of the seats is just for our coats and Ms. Dorothea's hat—how do you like *that* peach cobbler?

Who's Ms. Dorothea? Why she's the manager of our group. She's also Galleria's mom, *and* the most original person we've ever met. With her is Galleria's dad, Francobollo Garibaldi. He's Eye-talian—from Italy!—and he just loves my holiday eggnog. Mr. Garibaldi speaks with this Italian accent that makes everything sound like a *hoot*. He is even funnier than our uncle Skeeter back in Houston, if you can believe that.

Our daddy is here, too—even though he seems a little peaked lately. Maybe it's because he wants to be with his girlfriend—High Priestess Abala Shaballa Bogo Hexagone. No, you're not seeing things. That's her name! And as strange as it is, she is even stranger. Angie and I don't like her one bit. Ever since she came into our daddy's life, he hasn't been the same—and we wish she would get on her broomstick and ride right out of it again! Luckily, tonight she had to go to a special coven meeting with her kooky flock of followers, so she isn't here at the concert.

Most of Dorinda's family is here with us— her foster mother, Mrs. Bosco, and her eleven foster brothers and sisters—including Gaye, who I told you about earlier. I can't remember all their names—except for Shawn, Nestor, Twinkie, Kenya, Chantelle, Topwe, and the oldest of the Bosco bunch—Monie (if she pokes her mouth out any farther, it's gonna drop on the floor like a platter!), who has brought along her boyfriend, Hector. Dorinda also invited her half sister, Tiffany, (who wants to be in our group, but can't sing a lick!). Last but not least, LaRonda, who goes to school at Fashion Industries East with Dorinda, Galleria, and Chanel, is also here. (Next year, we hope the rest of the Cheetah Girls will transfer to our school—LaGuardia Performing Arts Annex, which is the most competitive performing arts school in the city, and filled with Mariah wanna-bes.) LaRonda is here because we owed her a big favor, but that's a whole 'nother story.

The only person who *isn't* here at the concert with us (and should be) is Chanel's mom, Mrs. Juanita Simmons. Her boyfriend, Mr. Tycoon, is in town, and they went to an opera at Lincoln Center. Nonetheless, Chanel is obviously tickled pink about being out with us and having fun. Like I said earlier, she is walking on crutches, because she fell on her tailbone during a ballet school audition.

Yes ma'am, we should have seen that one coming. When we were in Houston for Thanksgiving, Chanel was practicing ballet at our mother's, and fell on her butt, spraining her ankle a little. Then, at the audition, she sprained it much worse, 'cuz there was no carpet on the floor to protect her. She fell on her butt, like I said—right in front of the people who were auditioning her. As bad as she hurt herself, I think the embarrassment hurt worst of all. Ever since then, we've been trying to help her get better. We even had to postpone putting on a showcase for Def Duck Records until Chanel's ankle heals.

"When is Mariah coming on? It seems like we've been waiting forever!" whines Nestor, Dorinda's eight-year-old foster brother. Finally, the lights go down, but we see that it's not Mariah Carey at all, but the opening act assembling onstage. Now I want to whine like

Nestor, because I feel so disappointed. It seems like we've been waiting forever for the "Rainbow Diva" to come onstage. (*Rainbow* is the name of one of her albums.)

The opening act is none other than that very "last year" group, The LoveBabiez, whose first single off their debut album—*Sweet Lullaby*—makes me wanna boohoo for Mariah. I just don't like this song at all—the lyrics are not original, and the harmony is too loud. All of us clap along to the LoveBabiez music anyway, because we are here to have a good time.

"Didn't that song go lead?" I scream into Galleria's ear.

"Actually, it went gold," Galleria screams back, correcting my mistake. "But we'll see if they still have the Midas touch next year, or if they end up somewhere sucking on their pacifiers."

Galleria is right. It seems like it's real hard to keep a music career going in this business, and that makes all of us real scared. We could get left out in the cold, like a bunch of wanna-be cheetah cubs searching for our next meal!

See, you have to understand the music business—every day there is a new singing group with a new batch of songs, climbing up the charts because they had a really good producer working with them. Then, just as soon as the song leaves the charts, people forget all about the group. That is, unless you have pipes like Mariah, or Christina Aguilera, or really know how to make an impression because you're so original—which is what I hope happens to the Cheetah Girls.

I mean, I think we sing real well, but the other thing we have on our side is that Galleria and her mom, Ms. Dorothea, know how to stick out in a crowd, so our whole image is real original. But we'll see what happens—it's still too early to tell.

"Those shorts they're wearing look like *Pampers*," Galleria shrieks in my ear. I chuckle along, but I don't want Galleria to strain her voice yelling like that. Our vocal coach, Drinka Champagne, is always on us about "carrying on," as she calls it, "for no reason."

After twenty minutes, the LoveBabiez finish their set and hop into their oversized strollers, which are pushed off the stage by nannies in short skirts.

"Well, they sure had a lot of gimmicks for their show is all I can say," I humph to my sister.

Angie throws me a look, like, "When is Mariah Carey coming on?"

The lights go down again, and everybody in the audience screams. This time, I hope the "Rainbow Diva" herself will appear, so that the amateurs can go home. We are so excited we can hardly stay in our seats. Galleria jumps up, clapping, and the rowdy boys in back of us scream, "Sit down, Tony the Tiger!"

I see the look on Galleria's face, and I know she is mad. We hate when people make fun of our cheetah outfits—especially Galleria, because she isn't having it. I grab her hand and motion for her to sit down, because I don't want her getting upset or causing a scene. I mean, Galleria is very outspoken. She would do something like stick her tongue out at the rowdy boys and snarl like a wildcat, even though I don't think she would embarrass us in front of Mrs. Bosco and our Daddy. Luckily, the "Rainbow Diva" *finally* floats onto the stage.

"Oooh, look at her gown," I moan out loud, because I'm so caught by surprise. Mariah is wearing a white, sparkly, sequin gown to the floor—the spotlight follows her onstage, and it makes her look just like a beautiful angel. Her hair is so long and pretty—like Galleria's, except she straightens it more than Galleria does.

Now Galleria is happy again. She flashes her braces and puts her hands in the air, pushing her palms to the sky to the beat of the intro music. I look down the row at Daddy and smile, just to make sure he's all right—and he smiles back. I'm so glad he came with us. I know he usually just likes to relax with his pipe after work, sitting in his reclining chair, listening to jazz music—that is, when he isn't spending time with his High Priestess, the most original "pecan nut" we've ever met!

When Mariah starts to sing, Angie grabs my hand. Mariah's voice just sends chills down my spine, because she can really work her range to upper registers that we don't even have! Sure, we have sung in church choirs since we were seven, but we don't have voices like hers. Actually, no pop singer in the whole world has a voice like Mariah's—except maybe old-school singers like Minnie Riperton, Sista Fudge, and Whitney Houston.

Galleria grabs my right hand and squeezes it. Now we all sing along to Mariah's opening song—"Heartbreaker"—which is from her

Rainbow album. Of course, we know each and every word to *all* her songs, because we listen to the radio all the time—which drives Daddy crazy. We try to explain to Daddy that we're not listening just for fun. Now that we're in a singing group, we have to stay on top of the game, and keep up with the latest songs. Daddy just shakes his head—if it isn't jazz or gospel, he thinks it sounds like "a whole lotta noise."

I look over at Mr. Garibaldi, and he is just beaming and clapping along. We wish Daddy could have a good time like that, but he doesn't—especially not since he and our mother have been dee-vorced. You'd think he would be happy that we came up here to live with him—and maybe he is, but Daddy has a strange way of showing his feelings.

An hour or more goes by, but it seems like five minutes. Mariah belts out song after beautiful song, and I'm in heaven just to be here.

"I wish our seats were closer to the stage," Angie mumbles in my ear. I throw her a look. Of course, I'm thinking the same thing, but I'm just grateful to be here—even if we are sitting way up in the third tier of seats.

"Yeah, I wish we could see her up close," I yell back, checking out all the musicians in her band—thirteen of them—and the beautiful, glittering balls suspended on the stage. "Maybe one day, we'll get to sit in the front row of a concert, but you've gotta admit, this beats the Karma's Children concert in Houston any old day!"

"Go, Mariah!" I scream for good measure, as she announces the last song she is going to sing. It's one of my favorites—"When You Believe"—the duet she did with Whitney Houston for the *Prince of Egypt* movie. All of a sudden, I realize that *my* voice is getting hoarse from yelling all night.

"I'm gonna have to drink hot tea with lemon as soon as we get home," I mumble to Angie, thinking about our vocal practice in the morning. Every Saturday, the Cheetah Girls take vocal and dance lessons at Drinka Champagne's Conservatory. And believe me, Drinka doesn't play, either—she can tell if we're not singing up to speed, or just being plain lazy—and she'll call us out in front of everybody!

After clapping a thousand times (my hands are sore, too), the lights go up, and we all stand up and start putting on our coats. I beam at Galleria, and I know we're thinking the same thing—and we're not even twins!

"I wonder how we're gonna get backstage?" Galleria ponders out loud. "I guess it can't go any worse than our Karma's Children dismiss." After that concert, the security guards gave us the bum's rush, not even letting us near Karma's Children's dressing room—even though we were one of the opening acts!

"I know that's right," I say, shrugging my shoulders.

"Well, I don't care. I swear this time we're gonna 'bum rush' the situation into a celebration," Galleria says, beaming her big smile

"That's fine with me, too," I reply, wondering how I'm gonna explain this to Daddy.

"That's fine with me three," Dorinda adds, now that she's in on our conversation.

"Was that off the hook, snook, or what?" Galleria says, beaming again.

"You can say that again," Angie says, putting her arm through mine.

"I hope we get to perform here one day—the Cheetah Girls at Madison Square Garden." Galleria has that starry-eyed look that makes her, well, someone special. "And wait till you see the security guards who'll be guarding *us*—they're gonna make those Mighty Men in Houston look like lunch meat!"

"I know that's right," I say again. When Galleria gets that look in her eyes, you know something good is about to happen, because there is no stopping her determined ways.

I just wonder when something is gonna happen with our group. With Chanel being on crutches, we don't want to push anything, but Def Duck Records did say they were going to put us in the studio with producer Mouse Almighty to cut a few songs for a demo. It's been a long time since we got a call from them—and we've all been getting anxious that they've forgotten about us.

"Have you heard a little something from Mouse Almighty?" I ask hesitantly, because I'm not sure if I even want to hear the answer.

"No. Just a whole lot of nothing," Galleria says, smirking like she's unhappy. "He's in the studio with Kahlua, working on her new album. Let's hope when he finishes, he won't forget about the five hungry cheetah cubs he promised to work with."

"Well, darling, people only remember the last bread crumbs you threw on the pond," Ms. Dorothea pipes up. "So you can bet Kahlua Alexander is putting every producing morsel that Mouse Almighty has to offer into her platinum-selling beak."

"I heard that," I chuckle. Ms. Dorothea always has a real interesting way of putting things. Maybe Mouse Almighty will be ready to work with some new talent after filling Kahlua's beak. We sure hope so.

"*Madonna*, what a voice. *Ché voce!*" Mr. Garibaldi says, putting his beaver hat on his head and prancing around happily.

"Madonna doesn't have a voice like that," Dorinda replies, thinking Mr. Garibaldi was comparing Mariah's voice to Madonna's.

"No, silly willy—'*Madonna*' is just an Italian expression," Galleria says, correcting Dorinda's blunder. "You know, like, 'Holy cannoli'—that type of shout-out."

"Word?" Dorinda says, scrunching up her cute nose in amusement. "I didn't know that—is that how Madonna got her name, then?"

"Absolutely, schnooky—she's Italian-American," Galleria says, grabbing Dorinda by the shoulders and practically picking her up off the floor. "Man, you hooked us up. We can't thank you enough—Do' Re Mi hooked up her posse!"

Galleria twirls poor little Dorinda right into this couple, but they just beam at us, digging Galleria's energy. We walk down from the steep rows of seats, but there are so many people that the crowd is moving slower than snails stuck in a mudslide. All we want to do is figure out how to get to the backstage area.

"You never know how things flow. I mean, we might just pull this abracadabra off without even breaking a sweat," Galleria says. But I know she is just trying to reassure us. The rest of us don't have Galleria's nerve. Truthfully, we get real nervous if we feel like people are rejecting us, and it seems like there are always a whole lot of people trying to keep you from doing things, or reaching your dreams.

"You really think we're gonna get to meet Mariah?" Tiffany asks, her blue eyes getting bigger. It seems like she is the biggest Mariah fan out of all of us. Dorinda says Tiffany's whole room is covered with Mariah, Christina Aguilera, and Limp Bizkit posters. Daddy would have a proper fit if we hung up posters like that in our room!

Galleria puts her arm around Tiffany and heckles, "Well, I don't know if we're gonna meet Mariah, but she is certainly gonna meet us!"

Chapter 2

Finally, after crawling through the crowd forever, we are on the ground floor of the arena, next to the concession area. Angie and I look longingly at the Mariah posters and T-shirts that are hanging up for sale.

"Don't sleep on the Mariah posters, y'all!" yells the vendor, holding up a T-shirt of Mariah in a blue bikini.

"You girls want one?" Daddy asks, and I almost fall out of my shoes.

"Yes!" Angie replies, before I can say anything.

I can't believe Daddy is letting us buy a poster! I wonder what he thinks we're gonna do with it—keep it rolled up underneath our bed?

"I hope you know that we're going to hang the poster up in our room—on our very nice, white walls," I start in, to see how Daddy responds.

"I figured as much. Just don't go overboard—one poster on the wall is more than enough," Daddy says sternly. "I must say, I rather enjoyed her singing, though."

I think Daddy has almost cracked a smile. If I didn't know better, I'd say he has a crush on Mariah, the way he is staring at the poster! Boy, we sure are glad Dorinda invited us to this concert!

I whisper in Daddy's ear so Dorinda doesn't hear me. "Daddy, maybe we can have Dorinda's family over for dinner one night— you know, as a thank-you?"

"Well, as long as you girls are doing the cooking, I don't see why not," Daddy says. "Maybe after I finish redoing the living room."

"Redoing the living room?" I repeat, shocked right down to my shoes. Daddy just spent *six months* decorating the apartment! There's not a spot or a dot anywhere, and *nothing* is out of place. What on earth is he talking about?

"Abala felt it could use a little cultural warmth, so we're going to do it together,"

Daddy says, beaming. "She's taking me to a dealer in African arts and textiles on Sunday."

Now I *know* Daddy's been "touched by a cuckoo," because he can't possibly mean it! Angie looks at me like, "What is going on?" All of a sudden, Madison Square Garden is turning into Madison "Scare" Garden, and Halloween is long past! I mean, isn't it bad enough that we have to look at that ugly Bogo Mogo Hexagone Mask hanging in the hallway—the one Abala gave Daddy as a present?

"Daddy, are you okay?" I ask, noticing the gray cast to his complexion. I wonder why I didn't notice it before—maybe because the lights are so bright here.

"I can't say I'm feeling up to speed, but maybe it's the weather," Daddy says, wiping the tiny beads of sweat forming on his forehead. "I'm gonna get a lot of rest this weekend, that's for sure."

What I know for sure is, those herbs that High Priestess Abala Shaballa has Daddy taking aren't doing him one bit of good! I get this strange feeling in my chest, which I try to ignore. I just hope those herbs aren't hurting Daddy.

See, when Abala comes over, she has Daddy drinking all these herb drinks, to the point where he doesn't even eat regular food anymore. She gave him all these herbs to take at night, too—including frightshade, fenugreek, and some other odd names I can't pronounce!

While he is paying for our poster, I whisper into Angie's ear, "We are throwing those herbs on his nightstand right into the garbage!"

Angie nods her head, and I know we have a plan. There is no stopping us when we put our heads together.

All of a sudden, I realize we haven't paid much attention to Chanel—and we don't want her feeling left out of everything just because she's hobbling on crutches. Of course, Ms. Dorothea has that situation under control: she is tending to Chanel like she's the most delicate cabbage in the patch.

"Excuse me, sir, could you not lean over her?" Ms. Dorothea commands a man who is trying to reach a poster. "Chanel, darling, don't move—from the looks of this buffalo herd, you could become one terribly trampled cheetah!" Ms. Dorothea holds up a tiny Mariah T-shirt, and asks Galleria, "Do you think this is too small for Toto?" Toto is their precious little dog—who eats better than we do!

"His butt will stick out!" Galleria giggles.

"That's the general idea, isn't it?" Ms. Dorothea snipes, then pays for Toto's latest fashion item.

"How does your ankle feel?" I ask Chanel, concerned.

"I can't wait to get rid of these crutches!" she huffs.

"Don't worry, *mamacita*, you'll be flying like Mary Poppins in no time," Galleria says. She helps Chanel balance on her crutches while she peers at the poster near the top of the display.

"Oooh, look at the Butterfly T-shirt," Twinkie exclaims, pointing at the T-shirt stand. I feel bad that Dorinda's foster brothers and sisters can't get T-shirts—but at twenty dollars each, they can't afford them.

"You just love butterflies, don't you?" Tiffany asks Twinkie.

"I wish I was a butterfly and I could fly away!" Twinkie replies.

"Did you like the concert?" I ask her.

"Oh, yeah—can we meet the Butterfly

Lady?" Twinkie asks, her innocent blue eyes opening wider.

"Well, we're gonna try—if Mrs. Bosco doesn't mind," Galleria says firmly, grabbing Twinkie by the hand.

"That's all right with me," Mrs. Bosco says. "I think Gaye's having a good time, so let's keep going."

Gaye just stands there, quiet. I think it's the least we can do for her. She might not know who Mariah Carey is *now*, but maybe when she gets bigger, it'll be something nice to remember—instead of all the painful memories she's gonna have when she grows up and finds out that her mother abandoned her in a playground.

"Sir, how do we get backstage?" I ask the T-shirt vendor.

The vendor gives us directions. Then I squeeze Angie's arm, which is locked into mine, and yell, "Come on, y'all—this caravan is moving south!"

If we thought the security guards at the Karma's Children concert in Houston were mean, then the ones guarding the backstage area in Madison Square Garden are big ol' bulldogs who missed their mealtime! We haven't even gotten past the backstage door when one of the security guards, with biceps the size of whole turkeys, barks out, "Please, exit to the right!"

All of sudden, Angie and I feel like the Lion in *The Wizard of Oz*—two weaselly cowards without enough courage to spread on a split-pea sandwich! We stand there, speechless, frozen in our tracks.

"Let's just leave," Dorinda's older foster sister Monie blurts out to her boyfriend, Hector. "Dorinda, we're gonna bounce."

"Why don't we just wait and see what happens?" Hector says quietly.

"What for?" Monie snaps at him, sucking her teeth. "They ain't gonna let us back there, so let's just go."

Hector whispers to her again, but this time I can't hear what he's saying.

"*No*—let's just *go*!" Monie insists, and I can tell she's gonna win this argument.

We look over at Dorinda, and she raises her eyebrows, like, "Here we go again—another showdown at another rodeo." I feel sorry for Dorinda—it must be hard, sharing a bedroom with that sourpuss Monie. At least Angie and I get along like two peas in a pod—even though she tries to sneak up in my shoes sometimes, or puts holey stockings back in our sock drawer.

"Bye, Mrs. Bosco—thank you for inviting us," Monie says to her foster mother.

"Don't thank me—thank Dorinda," Mrs. Bosco corrects her. Good for Mrs. Bosco, sticking up for poor Dorinda! See, Mrs. Bosco had told Dorinda she could invite whomever she wanted. If it was me, I sure would have run out of tickets before I picked Monie's name out of the grab bag. God would've had to forgive me for that one!

"I already told her thank you," Monie says, getting a snip of an attitude—more than Daddy would ever allow, that's for sure.

I sneak a look at Daddy, but he is engrossed in conversation with Mr. Garibaldi. Daddy looks grayer and more tired than ever, and I start feeling worried all over again. Besides, Dorinda's younger foster brothers and sisters seem like they're getting fidgety. Maybe we should all go home.

"I'll see y'all later," Monie says, waving good-bye to me and Angie without even cracking a smile.

"Good-bye, sourpuss," I want to yell after her—but of course I don't.

Now LaRonda, Dorinda's friend from school, has lost her courage too. "I told my mother I'd be home at eleven, and I gotta go all the way to the Bronx," she says, shifting her weight like she's kinda nervous.

"It's not even ten yet!" Dorinda pleads.

"I know, but I don't want to cause any problems. I really appreciate you inviting me to the concert," LaRonda says, trying to be real nice but backing out.

"Awright," Dorinda whines, kissing her good-night on the cheek instead of pulling her cowardly tail.

"Mariah was off the hook," LaRonda says, brightening. Then she turns to Galleria. "Wait till I tell Derek Hambone on Monday—he's gonna be too through with you!"

Derek is this boy at their school who likes Galleria. He joined our social club, Kats and Kittys, just so he could hang with us.

"Ooo, you're *terrible*!" Chanel says, catching LaRonda's drift.

"Now we've gotta slay this dragon," Galleria says, motioning her head in the direction of the security guard—who looks like he has had more than his share of Hungry Man dinners.

"Ladies, you cannot block the entrance, please exit door right!"

Peering up at the security guard from under her big cheetah hat, Ms. Dorothea barks back, "We're guests of Mariah Carey—which way is her dressing room?"

"That way!" the security guard motions without cracking a smile.

Whew.

"Leave it to Mom to find the yellow brick road," Galleria whispers in my ear.

"She could slay a dragon with that hat if she wanted to," Daddy says, smiling with satisfaction.

"Yes she could!" I beam back at Daddy, surprised that he cracked a joke. That's so unlike him! I'm surprised he's even going along with this whole backstage caper. Daddy doesn't like cat-and-mouse games, if you know what I mean. In other words, he's awfully strict. Ms. Dorothea, on the other hand, is more our cup of mint julep tea—she likes to have fun, but she takes care of business, too.

Snaking through the crowd and going up two flights of stairs, we find ourselves in another long hallway, with a row of security guards in business suits lined up in front of us.

"Oh, boy—just when we thought we were on the yellow brick road," hisses Galleria as we approach one of them. We all huddle together, like a swarm of nineteen bees in search of a bee-hive. "Maybe Mrs. Bosco'd better ask him."

"I'll ask," Mrs. Bosco offers, pulling Gaye to her side. I think Gaye is scared now, because she starts sucking her thumb. "Excuse me, would it be possible to have a word with Ms. Carey? She invited us," Mrs. Bosco tells one of the guards. "Or rather, her charity did."

Dorinda looks at me, embarrassed.

"Her charity?" the security guard says, look-ing puzzled. Angie and I are so embarrassed, we just look at his navy blue suit.

"Darling, we're Ms. Carey's guests—could you ask if we can see her?" Ms. Dorothea says, jumping in.

"I'm sorry, but all these other people are waiting for Ms. Carey too, and we're not letting anyone else in," the bodyguard says. I notice that he has one of those ear things on.

"Certainly—we can wait here with the other people. There's no harm in that, now, is there?

Just in case?" Ms. Dorothea continues.

"Suit yourself. I'm gonna have to ask you to please step aside, though."

I wonder how people can be so mean . . . I hope *I* never have a job where I get to be nasty to people all day!

I can tell that Dorinda is still embarrassed. "Maybe we should just go," she says to her foster mother.

Much to our surprise, Mrs. Bosco retorts, "Ms. Dorothea is right. We waited this long— what's it gonna hurt to wait a little longer? You know I ain't cooking dinner tonight when we get back home, so I'm a free agent!"

"But next Sunday night, I expect all of you at *our* dinner table," Mr. Garibaldi pipes up.

"Yeah!" Twinkie says, jumping up.

"I'll have to ask my parents," Tiffany says, looking at Dorinda.

"What are we gonna eat?" Topwe blurts out, causing the rest of the kids to giggle.

They must be awful hungry. Even though we had dinner before we left for the concert, *I* could eat another meal right now—and I'm sure I ate more for dinner than they did!

"Daddy makes lobster fra diavolo every

Sunday night—you know, it's like a family tradition," Galleria says, looking down at Topwe. He is wearing a white shirt, with a cute little burgundy bow tie that makes him look like a little gentleman. It must be so hard, dressing all these kids every morning!

"Does the lobster bite?" Nestor asks, grinning at his joke. He's a little younger than Twinkie, and has lots of pretty, curly brown hair. I wonder how he got to be in a foster home. . . . We never ask Dorinda anything about the kids unless she tells us—and she doesn't tell us much, that's for sure.

Chapter

3

We stand outside Mariah's dressing room for ages. We feel worst for Chanel, because it can't be good for her sprained ankle and tailbone to be standing so long on her crutches. Of course, she'll never admit any such thing, but that's just Chanel for you—she never lets on when she's hurting. You'd think the bodyguards outside of Mariah Carey's dressing room would have some sympathy for a poor girl on crutches!

"How long are they gonna keep us waiting in line, like wolves in the cold waiting for a Happy Meal?" Galleria hisses, then snuggles up to her mother.

As if Glinda the Good Witch heard Galleria's

whine, the dressing-room door opens, and a lady with a clipboard steps into the hallway. We look at her like she's the ticket to our next meal. Feeling our eyes on her, she turns and smiles at Ms. Dorothea. (Daddy is right, Ms. Dorothea's cheetah hat sure does come in handy for emergencies!)

"Um, Miss, do you think you could help us?" Ms. Dorothea asks the lady.

"I don't know, but I'll see," the lady responds hesitantly, like she hopes she didn't open the box with the booby prize inside.

Ms. Dorothea whispers in the lady's ear.

"Oh, I see—well, the tickets were extended through Mariah's charity organization," the lady continues, "and we can't extend any further invitation beyond that."

"Yes, yes, we understand," Ms. Dorothea says. She pauses, then adds, "Look, do you know how much it would mean to poor little Gaye, here, just to get a picture with Mariah? You know all about her situation, don't you?"

"I understand, Ms. . . ."

"Just call me Dorothea, darling. What do you think—could you give it a whirl?"

We can tell the lady is warming up to Ms.

Dorothea, just like everybody else does. "I'll see what I can do," she says. "But you see all these people on line—they're invited guests of Mariah's, so I really can't promise you anything."

The lady walks away, and Galleria starts to chuckle. "Mom, you are just shameless."

"Well, shame on *her* for not inviting us in *immediately*!" Ms. Dorothea huffs.

"Back to the waiting game," I moan, leaning on the wall and getting comfortable again.

"Sing a song for us, Tiffany," Chanel says to Dorinda's half sister.

Poor Tiffany looks like a deer caught in the headlights. Lord forgive us, but we would rather be chased by a wild pack of coyotes than have to listen to her sing another song—her voice is *terrible*!

"Why don't *you* sing the new song you wrote about Dorinda and me?" Tiffany answers, smirking. "Bet you didn't know I knew about that one, huh, *mamacita*?"

That really gets us laughing—but not for the reason Tiffany thinks. She sounds so funny when she tries to talk like Dorinda and Chanel! Tiffany opens her pink knapsack and pulls out a pack of Twinkies—the third pack she's eaten since we've been at the concert! Since we're all pretty hungry, we stare at the Twinkies like they're lamb chops dripping with mint jelly!

"You want one?" Tiffany asks Nestor, who seems like he's gonna chomp it right out of her hand.

"Yeah!" he says, grateful.

"Okay, so lemme hear you sing the song," Tiffany says, not letting us off the hook.

"Okay, here's our song—I wrote it especially for you and Miss Dorinda," Galleria says, motioning for us to get into singing formation. "Are you ready, Cheetah Girls?"

"Ready for Freddy," I reply. And we start to sing:

"Dorinda's got a secret
and it's cutting off her flow
(Is that right, girlita?)
According to our sources,
She thought we didn't know
(Kats and Kittys, you'd better take notes)
Today for the first time (the very first time)
Do' Re Mi found out that she's not alone
(What are you saying?)
She found out she's got a sister
And it's making her moan and groan!

> *Do' Re Mi on the Q.T.*
> *Do' Re Mi on the D.D.L.*
> *(That ain't swell)*
> *Do' Re Mi on the Q.T.*
> *Do' Re Mi on the D.D.L.*
> *(Why won't you tell?)"*

Dorinda's foster brothers and sisters are clapping along, and they seem to enjoy it as much as the other people waiting outside Mariah's dressing room. Tiffany is beaming from ear to ear, too.

See, Galleria whipped up the lyrics to this particular song after Dorinda met Tiffany for the first time. Tiffany had found out she was adopted, and had a half sister in foster care, so she went and tracked Dorinda down. I can't imagine what it must have felt like to have a sister suddenly pop up out of nowhere—and a white sister at that!

It must be real confusing for Dorinda sometimes, to keep up with all that goes on in her family life. Anyway, Dorinda didn't tell us about meeting Tiffany—not until Tiffany showed up at the Battle of the Divettes competition at the Apollo Theatre and waited for us outside. (There is always some drama going on with the Cheetah Girls, that's for sure.)

"Wow, you are such a dope songwriter!" Tiffany exclaims to Galleria.

"Well, thank you, *mamacita*!" Galleria riffs back, imitating Tiffany.

"You girls are good!" says this lady wearing a caftan—kinda like the ones Daddy's girl-friend, High Priestess Abala Shaballa, wears.

"Yes, we have a singing group called the Cheetah Girls," I tell the lady proudly. Usually Galleria is the one who speaks for us, but it feels good speaking out myself for a change.

"Are you waiting for Mariah?" the lady continues. "Is she gonna help you?"

Now I feel embarrassed, and the words get stuck in my throat.

"No, we're just here on a social tip," Galleria says, piping up.

Suddenly I feel stupid. Galleria is always the one who knows just what to say to people. Just like her mother.

"I design the dancers' costumes, so let me know if you need any work done," the lady goes on to explain.

"Our manager makes our costumes," Galleria says proudly, pointing to Ms. Dorothea.

"Oh, is that right?" the lady says, like she's embarrassed. Then she heaves a deep sigh. "I wish they would hurry up so I can get Mariah to sign her album for my grandson—he just loves her to death."

"We do too!" Tiffany blurts out. "Maybe you can help us meet her."

Dorinda seems uncomfortable about what Tiffany's said. "Well, maybe we'll just go home after all—it is getting late."

Just then, the door to Mariah's dressing room opens again, and the lady with the clipboard motions for Ms. Dorothea. She whispers something in her ear, and the next thing we know, it's like Moses parted the Red Sea—because we're being ushered inside!

I grab Angie's hand real tight. "We can stay for five minutes," Ms. Dorothea whispers to us. On that cue, Galleria pulls her camera out of her bag, and we move our caravan forward. Mrs. Bosco motions to Nestor and Shawn to keep everybody quiet. We are so excited we can hardly stand it. My heart is thumping in my chest!

When we get inside Mariah's dressing room

(which feels like it's half the size of the arena), the first thing we see is millions of flowers. At first we don't see Mariah, because a crowd of people are fussing around her. "She has to go to the Angel Ball as soon as she leaves here," the clipboard lady tells Ms. Dorothea.

Now I catch a glimpse of Mariah—she is wearing a beautiful pink taffeta gown covered in silk butterflies!

"I bet you that's a Dolce & Gabbana gown," Galleria says, eyeing it carefully. Galleria knows a whole lot of stuff about fashion that Angie and I don't—but we sure can tell from here that the gown looks like "diva material."

We wait quietly until the lady motions for us to be introduced to Mariah. Mrs. Bosco is introduced first, and Mariah's face beams brightly as she shakes Mrs. Bosco's hand and looks at Gaye. She bends over to talk to Gaye, but Gaye tries to hide behind Mrs. Bosco's dress. Mariah stands there like a statue, and finally Gaye looks at her. "Hi, Gaye," Mariah says softly.

Gaye stretches out her arms for Mariah to hug her. I feel the tears forming in my eyes. After they finish hugging, the lady introduces us to Mariah. I am so nervous, I can't even hear the sound of my voice.

"Thank you so much for coming," Mariah says to us. She is so pretty, we can't stop staring at her. I can't believe we are standing here with *Mariah Carey*!

"Um, girls, let me take a picture of you with Mariah—if that's all right with you, Miss Carey?" Ms. Dorothea asks. Thank goodness she knows how to be professional while we stand there gawking!

"Of course." The five of us stand with Mariah, and Ms. Dorothea takes a picture. Galleria motions for her to take another.

"Hold your horses, darling—I've been at this rodeo before," Ms. Dorothea chuckles as she snaps the second picture. That causes Mariah to giggle.

"Can we take one, too?" Nestor asks.

The lady with the clipboard motions for Mrs. Bosco and Dorinda's foster brothers and sisters to stand with Mariah, so that Ms. Dorothea can take a picture. After that, the lady tells us, "Ms. Carey has to get to the ball now. Thank you for coming."

"Thank you for singing!" Chantelle blurts out.

"You're welcome." Mariah beams at her.

"Um, excuse me—can my, um, sister take a picture with you, too?" Dorinda squeaks and looks at Tiffany.

The lady with the clipboard is trying to be nice, so she lets Tiffany and Dorinda take a picture with Mariah. Tiffany is grinning more than the Easter Bunny does when he's delivering his eggs. I mean, she is grinning so much, her cheeks are red!

When we get back outside Mariah's dressing room, we look at the people standing there waiting, and we feel like we've won the lottery! The lady with the clipboard tells the security guard that no one else will be allowed into the room, because Mariah has another engagement to attend.

"What is the Angel Ball?" Galleria asks her mom as we walk away. "Sounds like we should be there."

"If you had a thousand dollars to buy a ticket, you could attend, darling," Ms. Dorothea quips.

"A thousand dollars?! What kind of ball is it?" Chanel asks.

"It's a charity benefit, thrown by songwriter Denise Rich, and all the monies raised are donated to cancer research," Ms. Dorothea explains. "Ms. Rich's daughter died of cancer at a young age."

"I can't wait till we can go to balls," Chanel says wistfully.

"As long as you don't pirouette down the red carpet, Chuchie," Galleria riffs, reminding Chanel how she injured herself. "I can't wait to see the pictures we took with Mariah."

"Can you get the film developed tomorrow?" Dorinda asks Galleria.

"I'm on it, doggone it," Galleria heckles. "I know *you* can't wait to get your grubby little paws on the photo ops!" When we went to Houston, Dorinda bought a cheetah photo album, and she is now officially the keeper of the Cheetah Girls scrapbook.

"Can I have a copy too?" Tiffany asks nervously. "I want to show it to my mom. She's not gonna believe I got a picture with Mariah Carey!"

"A picture is worth a thousand memories," Ms. Dorothea says, beaming at us.

"This one's gonna be worth more like a *trazillion*!" Galleria heckles.

"And a whole lot more!" Angie says, joining in the afterglow.

Once we get to the street, we kiss each other

good night. "See you in the morning," I yell after Galleria, Chanel, and Dorinda.

"See you later, *mamacitas*!" Tiffany shouts after me and Angie. Mr. Garibaldi is dropping Tiffany off at home, and she sure seems happier than a pig in a poke.

"Daddy, I think we should plaster our bedroom with copies of the photos, don't you?" I kid him as we climb into a cab.

"Let's just start with the poster, and we'll see," he says calmly.

It sure is hard getting a rise out of him. I guess he's older, so he doesn't know what it means to us, to meet someone as important as Mariah Carey.

Almost as if reading my mind, he pipes up, "I'll never forget the time I saw Miles Davis playing at Smokey Johnson's Cafe. Man, now *that* was something to see."

"When was that?" Angie asks.

"Oh, a long time ago, when I had another life—before y'all were born," Daddy says, like he's unsure of himself.

"What do you mean, 'another life?'" I ask.

"Just what I said—another life," Daddy says, and doesn't continue.

Angie and I look at each other, then shrug our shoulders. I guess he means when he was younger. He sure is acting strange tonight, though—not at all like himself. Maybe it's because he isn't feeling well.

"Did you like the concert?" Angie asks, yawning.

"Yes, I did—she sure is something special."

"She sure is. . . ." I say, closing my eyes and letting myself fall asleep.

When we reach our house, I wake up out of my stupor, and realize I was dreaming about the scary Bogo Mogo Warrior Mask that High Priestess Abala Shaballa gave Daddy as a present. It's this big ugly mask that looks like the head of a space alien, with bright-red marks across the cheeks. Daddy hung it up right at the foot of the stairs, so every time we go up or come down, it scares me to death.

High Priestess Abala says when the markings change colors, it means it's time for Hexagone to reign once again, and the world will become a more magical place. In the meantime, it's supposed to watch over us and keep away evil spirits. Well, I know *that's* not true, because High Priestess Abala is still here, hanging off Daddy like he's a prize she won at the county fair!

Up in our bedroom, Angie and I say our prayers, then tape our prized Mariah Carey poster up over the bureau. We stare at it from across the room in our twin beds, then turn off the night lamp.

"Can you help me with my math homework tomorrow?" Angie asks in the dark. I like math and chemistry more than she does, which is why I would make a good forensic pyschologist—because I like to analyze things to *death*.

"Yeah, I will," I sigh, then lay my head down on my pillow, thinking about what Daddy said to me at the Garden. "Daddy told me we can invite Dorinda and her family over for dinner—after he redecorates the living room with High Priestess Abala. Can you believe that?"

"Believe what—that he's gonna let eleven kids eat in our dining room?"

"No, that he's going to redecorate the living room!"

"No, I *can't* believe it!" Angie moans. "And I must say, I'm getting awfully worried about that woman coming around here too much. I don't like it one bit."

"Neither do I—and I don't see why she has to be all up in our business—after all the work Daddy did, and all the money he spent decorating this apartment the first time." I can feel myself getting more upset by the minute. "Daddy just doesn't seem like himself anymore."

"He sure doesn't," Angie says, concerned.

"Maybe that's why he's letting Abala talk him into bringing more ugly things into this house."

"We'd better mention it in our prayers," Angie says. And so we climb down from our beds and kneel on the floor to say our prayers—*again*.

"God, please don't let Daddy bring home any more Bogo Mogo Warrior Masks, or kooky decorations," I say.

Angie finishes the prayer for me. "Because we like everything just fine the way it is."

And then we both say, "Amen!"

Chapter 4

Of course, we can't wait to gloat to everyone at Drinka Champagne's Conservatory about our fabulous evening with Mariah Carey. We start in bragging as soon as we come through the door—with the receptionist, Miss Winnie. She has the same name as our deceased paternal grandmother, so you know we just love her to death—ha, ha, that's just a joke!

"You girls keep it up, and soon we won't be seeing any more of you," Miss Winnie says, peering over her silver-rimmed glasses. "You'll be sending us postcards from the road, complete with little red kisses in the corners!"

"Yeah, right—we haven't even heard a quack attack from Def Duck Records," Galleria says, waving her hand. "Now that Chanel is on crutches, it's just as well."

Poor Chanel looks sheepish when Galleria says this, but Miss Winnie doesn't say another bo-peep.

"Don't you worry, Miss Winnie, we won't be getting any big-headed ideas like that any time soon—not as long as I still need work on my upper register," huffs Dorinda.

"I know what you're saying," I say. Then I notice the hurt look on Dorinda's face.

"I'm not *that* bad," she huffs back at me.

"No, I didn't mean you—I meant *all* of us need practice!" I say, embarrassed that Dorinda took it the wrong way. I just hate to hurt anybody's feelings, least of all Dorinda's. From the beginning, she has been nothing but kind to me and Angie—even when Galleria and Chanel were making fun of us. (We've never said anything, but we know they used to call us "the Huggy Bear twins" behind our backs!)

Miss Winnie smooths over the situation quickly. "Honey, after hearing Mariah Carey sing, we all should practice for ninety-nine years before we even step up to a microphone and call ourselves cute."

In the House with Mouse!

I almost open my mouth to say, "I know what you're saying" again—but Angie pokes me in the side. Thank goodness my better half knows how to shut my mouth sometimes.

Luckily, Dorinda is chuckling right along with Miss Winnie. "Were you a singer, too?" she asks, curious.

"Was?" Miss Winnie says, primping her hair. "I *still* give them fever—in church, anyway."

"Hi, Miss Winnie," announces Danitra, one of the other students who takes vocal class with us. She has hot-pink hair, and is in a group called Think Pink.

"Hi, Danitra, how are you doin'?" I ask.

"I could puke," Danitra blurts out. "We just found out there's another group called Pink, and the lead singer has pink hair!"

"So go yellow, mellow," Galleria tells the poor girl.

Danitra waves her hand, and runs her fingers through her hair. "How are you doing, Chanel?" Danitra asks when she sees the crutches. It's the first Saturday since she had the accident that Chanel has been back to vocal practice.

"Fine!" Chanel says excitedly, then practically

attacks Danitra with her crutches as she tells her every last detail about the Mariah Carey concert.

"You did *not* get to meet her!" Danitra squeals with disbelief.

"*Sí, mamacita!*" Chanel counters. "You shoulda seen all the flowers in her dressing room, and the butterflies fluttering on her gown—not the one she performed in, but afterward." Chanel makes it sound like we went to the party with Mariah!

"How did you get free tickets?" Danitra asks, still trying to figure out if we are telling a fib-ulous tale. If you ask me, I think Miss Pink-haired Danitra has been bitten by the green-eyed monster.

I just hope Chanel doesn't blurt out the truth. Dorinda is already mad enough at us for telling everybody at Kats and Kittys about her foster home situation. See, at our last meeting, the Kats members voted for Dorinda's foster mother, Mrs. Bosco, to receive a charitable donation from our volunteer fund, to be used for Gaye's welfare. Dorinda almost blew a gasket afterward. We felt terrible.

Luckily, we are saved by the bell—or rather, by the director of the conservatory herself—the former disco diva, Miss Drinka Champagne. "I see you girls are getting into the mix with your usual tricks," Miss Drinka says, chuckling, when she sees us cackling with Danitra.

We immediately straighten up our act, because Miss Drinka is very particular about professional behavior from her students—inside and outside the studio.

"Tell Drinka, darlings—mother wants to sip *every* detail, right down to Mariah's manicure!" Drinka flings her hand at us, and flashes her foot-long red claws. Whenever we think her outfits can't get any more, well, creative, Drinka outdoes herself again. Today, she's wearing red cigarette-leg pants with a matching bustier, and a cape with pom-poms and jingle bells hanging off it.

"That girl has octaves to spare," Drinka says, stomping down the hallway with us.

"We had twenty-five people in our posse!" Galleria boasts, listing everyone who came with us to the concert.

"Even our father came," I tell Drinka. She met our father once, when he came to pick us up. He just wanted to see what the conservatory was like, since he pays for our training.

"How is that handsome father of yours?" Drinka asks, her dark, dramatic eyes sparkling up a storm.

"He's fine," I say.

Don't tell me that the legendary disco queen, Drinka Champagne, likes *our father*! All of a sudden, I'm feeling disappointed inside. Why couldn't Daddy pick someone dope for a girl-friend, like Drinka Champagne? They still love her in places like Japan, and in Holland, where people tend to be more liberal-minded than we are in the States. At least if Drinka were his girl-friend, we would have some fun! She would be like a "fairy stepmother" or something. But no, Daddy has to go and meet the kookiest bird in the flock, and she has to fly her broomstick right to our house!

"Excuse me for a second, dolls," Drinka says, hurrying toward her office. "Get inside the studio—I'll see you in a New York minute."

We continue our bragging in the studio, and everyone wants the juicy details—everyone, that is, except for this tall, skinny guy in snake-skin pants (skinnier at the bottom than Drinka's) and matching jacket. We've never seen him before, and he just eyes us kinda coolly, then turns away. Another group of guys is huddled in the corner as Wolfman Lupe, the pianist, sits down on the piano bench and waits for the rest of the class to file in.

"Knucklehead alert, dead ahead," Galleria mumbles under her breath, nodding at the group of guys in the corner.

"I don't know . . . they look kinda cute," Chanel grins back. "So does the guy in the snakeskin pants."

"Oh, you *would* think so," Galleria whispers. "Let's just hope he doesn't hiss and bite."

Chanel grins right at the guy in the snakeskin pants, and he walks over to her. I guess it must help, using crutches—people think you're helpless or something. Boys never walk over to me and Angie when we smile. It always seems that guys like Galleria and Chanel anyway, because they're real pretty. Angie and I try not to let it bother us. Not that boys don't look at us—they do, sometimes—but we're not supposed to look at boys until we're sixteen, or Daddy will bury us alive!

"Hi, I'm Eddie Lizard," the skinny boy says to Chanel, flashing a beautiful smile.

Dag on, his teeth are white! I don't even realize

I'm staring at him, until he introduces himself to me, too. "Oh, hi—I'm Aquanette," I say, trying to snap myself out of it.

"Eddie Lizard," he says.

"We've never seen *you* before—we would have noticed," Chanel says, grinning.

I think Galleria must have poked Chanel in the back or something, because she seems like she's losing her balance on her crutches for a second. "That's okay, I don't need any help," she says, as Eddie Lizard extends his hand.

"I just moved here from Los Angeles," he says, folding his arms across his chest, which makes him seem very mysterious and mature. I guess he must be a little older than us—maybe in tenth or eleventh grade.

"*We've* been to Los Angeles!" I exclaim excitedly, but Eddie keeps looking at Galleria and Chanel.

"Oh, yeah?"

Galleria tells him all about our trip to Hollywood—performing in the Def Duck Records Showcase at the Tinkerbell Lounge, and staying at the Royal Rooster Hotel. If I didn't know any better, I'd think she was trying to make him like her—even though Galleria doesn't have to try very hard. *All* the boys like her.

Now I realize that Eddie *does* look familiar—and maybe that's why I've been staring at him (well, I'm sure not gonna admit that I think he's very cute. No, ma'am—especially since he doesn't seem the least bit interested in me!) *Where have I seen his face before?*

"Are you a singer?" Dorinda asks him, curious.

"No . . . well, yes—well, not exactly," Eddie Lizard says, like he's confused. He nervously toys with a silver talisman, shaped like a heart, dangling on a chain around his neck. I wonder if it's some kind of lucky charm or something. He does seem kinda mysterious. "I'm an actor, but I want to get vocal coaching, and my Dad used to know Drinka Champagne back in the day—so I came here, because everyone says she's the best."

"That she is," I reply, wondering if his dad is a singer or an actor too.

"Is that your real name—Eddie Lizard?" Galleria asks, smirking.

"Yes, it is. My father's name is Doktor Lizard," Eddie explains.

"Oh, he's a *doctor*—like a forensic pyschologist?" I ask, getting excited. Angie and I want to be doctors when our singing careers are over. I want to be a Chief Medical Examiner, and examine corpses for autopsy clues, and Angie wants to be a neurosurgeon, and operate on people's brains.

"Well, he's not *that* kind of doctor—um, it's spelled D-o-k-t-o-r Lizard. He's a hoodoo practitioner. He was the consultant on the movie *Vampire Voodoo Voyage*—maybe you saw it?"

"Are you kidding? We *love* horror movies!" Angie says excitedly.

"I played one of the corpses who falls in love with the voodoo queen Marie Fangella," Eddie says, chuckling.

"*That's* where I saw you!" I say excitedly. "I didn't recognize you with your eyeballs still in your sockets!"

"Oh, right, that was a good makeup job," Eddie chuckles in his soft way. "Now my dad is here in New York, curating the hoodoo exhibit at the African-American Museum. I, um, live with my dad, so we'll be here for a few months."

I wonder where his mother is. . . . It sure seems like we have a whole lot in common. All of a sudden, I feel something for a boy I've never felt before—except maybe for Major

"Beethead" Knowles, who tried to get my attention when I was ten years old by throwing a rock at me. He made me fall off the swing instead, and I ended up with a big gash in my left knee. Our grandmother, Big Momma, made Beethead swear he would never talk to us again, and he didn't—until we saw him in Houston on Thanksgiving this last trip.

"Is hoodoo like voodoo?" Dorinda asks, curious.

"Um, yes, it is from the same tradition—but it's practiced more in the United States. *Voudoun*, or voodoo, as you call it, was formed in Haiti," Eddie says nonchalantly.

Now Chanel looks at Eddie, really impressed. I wonder who he likes more—Galleria or Chanel—and I still can't help wishing it was me!

"I know all about Santeria and *brujeria*!" Chanel says proudly.

"Really?" Eddie asks her, getting more intrigued by the second.

"I'm Dominican and Cuban," Chanel explains.

All of a sudden, Drinka claps her hands loudly, waking us out of our cozy little chat with the Lizard. "Enough chatting and batting lashes ladies—it's time to get to work."

We all move to the center of the studio to begin our vocal warm-ups. All during the warm-ups, I'm wondering if I should tell Eddie Lizard about High Priestess Abala Shaballa. No, then he'll think I like him or something, I decide. I'd better just get all of this nonsense out of my head. *Too bad, because he sure is cute. Real cute.*

After vocal class, I grab my cheetah backpack and head for the door. I notice that Galleria is lingering inside the studio, and feeling around in her backpack like she's looking for something.

"You lost something?" I ask. But I already know the answer—she's just trying to get Eddie's attention! It works, too. After a few minutes, Eddie makes his way over to Galleria, and they are chatting with each other as we all walk to the elevator. Galleria is telling him all about the Cheetah Girls—but it doesn't look like she needs any help from us!

"The record company—Def Duck—you know, the same label that Kahlua Alexander is on—said they'd put us in the studio with producer Mouse Almighty. We're supposed to cut a few songs for a test demo or single, but we haven't heard a peep yet," Galleria laments like a damsel in distress.

Eddie acts like he's real interested in our music group, but I can tell he's even more interested in Galleria. Once we're outside, the two of them are stuck together like Popsicles—standing in front of the building, gabbing, while the rest of us just look on.

"You are mad funny," Eddie Lizard riffs, as Galleria tells him about our Cheetah Girls escapades in Hollywood.

I wonder if we're going to eat lunch together, like we usually do after Drinka's vocal class. I decide right then and there that I'm not going if the Lizard joins us. Why does it always seem like Galleria is the rooster with something to crow about? Well, that's not exactly true—'cuz the Cheetah Girls would've never gotten to Houston if it wasn't for me and Angie.

I throw Angie a look, like, "Let's go home." She just stands there, like she's mesmerized by this horse and pony show.

"Man, I went on so many auditions before I even got a gig as an extra in a crowd scene," Eddie laments, talking about his struggling acting career. I guess he wants Galleria to feel sorry for him, too.

"Really?" Galleria asks, like he's so cute, she can't believe he wouldn't just walk onto a movie set and become an instant star!

All of a sudden, a homeless man wearing a plastic bag wrapped around his body runs up to us and screams, "Satan lives! Satan lives!"

The rest of our crew try to act like it's no big deal, but Angie and I almost jump off the sidewalk, because he scared us half to death!

"Yes, he sure does," Eddie chuckles at Galleria, like he sees things like that every day in Los Angeles. "New York is such a trip, isn't it?"

"It sure is, but I grew up here, so I'm in it for the ride on the Coney Island Cyclone!" Galleria riffs at him. "Where do you go to school?"

"Because I have to travel so much with my dad, and for acting, I have a private tutor. That way I'll be able to finish high school next year."

"Oh, so you got it like that?" Dorinda pipes up. "Is it hard?"

"You mean, studying with a tutor?" Eddie asks. "Yeah—I've always got a lot of homework assignments. But, hey, listen, I've gotta go meet my father at the museum by three o'clock. Do y'all wanna go eat something around here? Where can we get our grub on?"

"Well, we're gonna go home, y'all, 'cuz we have to help Daddy with the remodeling," I blurt out.

"Come on, Aqua—I know the two of you aren't passing up a trip to Atomic Wings—not the dynamic wing-eating duo!" Galleria riffs at me and Angie.

Suddenly, I feel myself wincing inside. I know Galleria is just being her usual self, but why does she have to embarrass us like that in front of Eddie Lizard? I mean, she makes it sound like Angie and I are bone-chomping bugaboos, with incisor-teeth like dinosaurs, or something country like that.

"Well, we're gonna cook something to eat at home," I respond. I'm trying to act normal, but I guess I'm just showing off. After all, one thing Galleria can't do is cook—not like me and Angie.

"Wish we were invited over!" Galleria says. But I know she's ready to head over to Atomic Wings and chow down on an order of Insanely Hot Chicken Wings, which is exactly the way *we* like to eat them.

Suddenly, I feel my mouth watering, but I decide I'm not going to back down. Out of the corner of my eye, I can see Angie looking at me like I'm crazy. "Come on, Angie, let's go," I mutter.

It's all right with me. Let Galleria hold court with Eddie without our interference. That's just fine and dandy with the fabulous Walker twins—a.k.a. the Hot Sauce twins, a.k.a. the Huggy Bear twins.

"Aqua, come on, let's stay," Angie whispers, holding my arm to keep me by her side.

"No, thank you, ma'am—the Huggy Bear twins are going to head uptown and help our father," I insist. I can see the surprised look on Galleria's face. Good. Now she knows that sometimes other people have feelings too!

"Don't go, Aqua!" Chanel says, her eyes pleading. Now I'm starting to feel a little silly for being jealous, but I'm not backing out. Big Momma says I'm stubborn, and this time, I don't mind living up to my reputation. Not one bit!

Chapter 5

When you're an identical twin, you kinda take for granted that your "other half" is gonna stick up for you all the time. But today, Angie is being real trifling—even after the way Galleria insulted us in front of that "scaly creature." I don't believe for one second that Eddie Lizard's father is a hoodoo practitioner, or whatever kind of bogus doctor he calls himself!

"I thought I'd seen it all, with the likes of High Priestess Abala Shaballa Hexagone and her kooky coven of misfits," I mumble to Angie, but she doesn't say one word.

I'll never forget the first time Abala brought her cronies over to our house: Bast Bojo, with the bald head and beady eyes; Hecate Sukoji, the only lady I've ever seen with no eyebrows; Rasputina Twia, the dwarf with the straggly-looking teeth. They sure are a motley-looking bunch!

Abala Shaballa brought them over one night to concoct a Vampire Spell, so that the Cheetah Girls would win the Apollo Amateur Hour contest. Well, we *lost*—even after drinking that dees-gusting brew, and performing the Bogo Mogo ritual with all of them!

The whole way back on the train to our house, I have my mouth poked out, and Angie doesn't say a word—until she decides to start some trouble.

"I can't believe the way you were staring at that boy," she mumbles as I put the key in our front door.

"I was *not* staring at him," I snap back.

"Yes, you were—and I can tell you're jealous because he likes Galleria and not you," Angie says, hurting my feelings.

All of a sudden, I realize that *Angie probably likes him too*! After all, we're twins, right?

"I don't care who he likes!" I say, calling her bluff, then decide I'm not going to help Angie with her math homework after all. It's her problem if she fails the test!

"Yes you do," Angie says, folding her arms across her chest. "No sense in lying to me, 'cuz I know better."

I'm going to get Angie *real* good for this. "So what if I do? It doesn't matter."

"It sure doesn't," Angie says.

I shoot her a look, because I wonder what she means by that. Not that I care anymore. Eddie Lizard can go eat a frog—and so can Galleria!

Knowing "Miss Show-off," right about now she's probably showing him all the songs in her Kitty Kat notebook, and licking chicken grease off her fingers. I hope she gets fried chicken skin stuck in between her braces! That'll make her look real cute in front of Eddie Lizard.

As I open the apartment door, I wonder why the lights are on. . . . Daddy is real particular about turning off every light when we're not in the room. I know he went out with High Priestess Abala Shaballa to the African Arts dealer to pick out some new decorations. At least, that's what he told us he was doing when we left this morning.

Angie marches straight into the kitchen, and I let out a big sigh. *Finally.* I just want to go eat some lunch, then listen to some music in my room and be by myself. I hope Angie finds something to do with herself instead of bothering me. I can't seem to shake the bad feeling I have in my chest.

I put my keys on the side mantel in the foyer, but I notice there isn't any mail there. Usually, Daddy leaves all the Saturday mail on the table, and goes through it over the rest of the weekend. Hmmm. Maybe he took the mail with him. I go back to the outside foyer, and I notice that our mailbox is jam-packed—Daddy didn't even open it!

I wonder why Daddy didn't get the mail. . . . Looking down on the floor, I realize that he didn't pick up his newspapers either, because *The Amsterdam News* and *The New York Times* are still lying where the delivery woman left them!

Daddy was probably so engrossed with High Priestess Abala Shaballa and her shenanigans that he didn't have time to read his morning newspaper in peace, while sipping his coffee and some dees-gusting shake whipped up in his new blender.

I'll bet Abala came over with a toolbox and a

tape measure, trying to figure out how she's gonna rearrange everything, then carted Daddy away to all these kooky home furnishing places where witches shop!

I put the newspapers and the mail on the side mantel, then head for the kitchen, and make myself a catfish sandwich from last night's leftovers. Plopping down at the dining room table, I ignore Angie completely. I open one of the newspapers to today's horoscope for my astrological sign—Virgo.

> *The unconditional love for which you yearn cannot be bought at any price, so don't be tempted to sell your soul to the devil. Watch out for sheep wearing wolves' clothing, and vice versa. It may not be Halloween, but many evildoers will cloak their wrongful actions in disguises you may not recognize. Due to unforeseen circumstances, now is the time to take action, despite naysayers.*

I wonder what "unforeseen circumstances" means? I almost forget that I'm mad at Angie, and open my mouth to ask her—then catch myself. She wouldn't know anyway. If *I* don't know something, *she* usually doesn't either.

"Can you believe Eddie Lizard is the same guy from *Voodoo Vampire Voyage*?" Angie says, biting into her catfish sandwich. She *would* make herself the same thing to eat as I did. "He looks a lot skinnier in person. His eyes are prettier than I would have thought, too."

"Of course they are, Angie—'cuz he didn't *have* any in the movie!" I respond.

Exasperated with my pesty sister, I go back to trying to figure out my horoscope. *"Watch out for sheep wearing wolves' clothing. . . ."* Suddenly I get alarmed. Maybe they're talking about Eddie Lizard! I wonder if that means I should forget about him. . . .

"What does the horoscope say—that you like him, and should just admit it?" Angie says, smirking and biting into her sandwich.

"Why don't you read it and find out?" I say, pushing the newspaper in front of her. I swear, if I had a can of Daddy's SWAT insect spray, I'd spray it right at her, and watch her squirm like a cockroach before it turns over on its back and croaks.

BAM! All of a sudden, we hear a loud crashing noise from upstairs. Angie jumps up from the table.

"What if it's a burglar?" I hiss at her, getting paranoid.

We know Daddy isn't home, so what else could that noise be? No wonder the lights were on!

"Let's go see if Mr. and Mrs. Elliot are home," Angie says, getting scared, too. Mr. and Mrs. Elliot are our neighbors. We live in a duplex apartment, and there are only a few other people who live in our brownstone building. We run to the front door, and Angie whispers, "Let's leave it open, just in case the burglar wants to run away!"

"No—that's stupid. We should lock him inside," I say.

"We can't lock the door from the inside—if we close it, he can still get out!" Angie hisses back at me in a hushed voice.

"Let's just go," I say, realizing she's right, this time. We run out the door, and head for the stairs in the hallway. Angie runs so fast, she almost trips me from behind, making me annoyed at her all over again.

I hope Mrs. Elliot is home! I don't smell that familiar odor of gingerbread cookies wafting into the hallway. Mrs. Elliot runs her own "cookie book" company, Delilah's Dish and Tell. She writes romance novels that come with a package of cookies, so you can eat and read at the same time. We usually see Mr. or Mrs. Elliot carting boxes up and down the stairs, and moving stuff into vans outside. Of course, when we need them the most, we don't see them.

I knock on the door impatiently, hoping somebody answers. "Come on, come on!" I mutter under my breath.

Finally, the door is opened by their housekeeper, Esmeralda, who hardly speaks any English. "Is Mrs. Elliot home?" I ask quickly.

"No home," Esmeralda responds, smiling. Now I wish Chanel were here, so she could speak Spanish to Esmeralda, and tell her how scared we are that there is a burglar in our apartment!

"Esmeralda, can you help us? Somebody broke into our apartment," I blurt out, knowing full well she's probably not going to understand one word of my mumbo jumbo. Sure enough, Esmeralda gives me a blank look, and opens her brown eyes wider.

"Come, please," I beg her, motioning for her to come downstairs with us. But she seems unsure of what to do.

"You want I come?" she asks, pointing downstairs.

"*Sí!*" Angie blurts out.

All the way downstairs, Esmeralda is blabbing at us in Spanish, and we are blabbing at her in English, and neither one of us understands the other.

My heart almost jumps out of my chest when we get to our apartment door and find it open. I fall back into Esmeralda, and I can see that I've scared *her* now.

Angie grabs my arm, almost causing me to jump out of my skin. "I left the door open, remember?" she whispers.

Now the *three* of us are scared to go inside the apartment. All of a sudden, my skin feels itchy and crawly, like I have lice, so I start scratching all over.

Angie opens the door all the way, and the two of us tiptoe into the foyer, standing still to see if we hear any more noise. Esmeralda is still standing on the welcome mat outside the door. I grab her hand and pull her inside. I'll bet *now* she understands exactly what we want her to do!

As I begin to climb the narrow, winding stairs to the upper floor of our duplex, something tells me to turn around and look at the Bogo Mogo Hexagone Warrior Mask. "Angie!"

I hiss, pointing to the ugly creation that has made my life miserable. "The markings have turned redder! Haven't they?"

"I guess," Angie says, sticking her face right next to the mask. "Yeah, they have!"

We begin our climb, and I try for the life of me to remember what High Priestess Abala Shaballa said. . . . *When the markings on the mask turn brighter, it will be time for Hexagone to rule the world again. . . .* I *think* that's what she said, but I'm still not sure what that means.

The three of us climb the narrow, winding stairs to the upper floor. Maybe Abala's idea of redecorating meant getting Daddy out of the apartment and taking our furniture! Everybody tells us people get robbed in New York a lot.

I peer back down the stairway and look over the living room. Well, everything downstairs seems to still be there—unless she's got some kooks coming back later to get the living room furniture.

I can feel my heart pounding as we walk into my room and look around. Then we walk into the bathroom—and lastly, into Daddy's room.

"It's Daddy!" Angie shrieks when she sees

him lying in the bed. She goes running up the bed to shake him—and steps on something that makes a cracking sound. The lamp from his nightstand is shattered on the floor! Daddy must've knocked it over, reaching for something.

"The phone is off the hook," I add, picking up the receiver and putting it back into its cradle.

Esmeralda lets out a shriek and points to the floor, babbling in Spanish. I can't see what she's pointing at, but I'm concerned about Daddy. I sit on the bed and call his name, but he doesn't answer. "Daddy, can you hear me?"

I get so scared that I shake him, until he lets out a moan.

"What's wrong, Daddy?" I ask, getting hysterical.

"Is that you, Mattie?" Daddy asks, rubbing his eyes and waking out of his unconsciousness. "I never meant to hurt you."

Mattie? "Who's Mattie?" I repeat out loud.

Daddy doesn't answer, because he isn't really conscious. I've never heard him mention that name before. And what does he mean by "I never meant to hurt you"?

"Daddy, what's wrong?" Angie asks, getting hysterical too.

"Lord, my stomach hurts, my head hurts," Daddy moans, holding his head.

"We should get him to a hospital," Angie shrieks.

Esmeralda grabs my arm, still babbling in Spanish. She is trying to show me something on the mantel. I notice there are all sorts of strange things there. . . .

"Someone has burned the black and red candles and left them sitting there," I call out to Angie. Daddy doesn't burn candles, so I know it couldn't be him—especially not without putting them on a plate or something first, so the melted wax doesn't mess up the wood.

Esmeralda picks something up from the mantel and presses it into my hand. "What is this thing?" I ask, looking at it puzzled. "It looks like a gingerbread man made out of muslin or something."

Esmeralda presses another one into my hand, and gets real excited, babbling away.

"We should call Chanel and see what Esmeralda is trying to tell us!" Angie says, taking the gingerbread people out of my hands and dropping them back on the mantel.

I figure Chanel is still eating lunch at Atomic

In the House with Mouse!

Wings with Dorinda and the lovebirds—Galleria and Eddie Lizard—so I try her cell phone. Dialing the number, which I know by heart, I can hear my own heart pounding.

"Hola!" Chanel says, answering the phone chirpily.

"Hello, Chanel. Are you with Galleria?"

"Sí, mamacita. Eddie is going to take us to see his father's hoodoo altar!" she says excitedly.

"Chanel, something is wrong with Daddy—and Esmeralda, the housekeeper next door, is here with us, and she doesn't speak English. She's trying to tell us something. Could you translate for us?" The words tumble out of my mouth like an avalanche.

"Well, you could at least say, 'Hello, *mamacita*,'" Chanel responds.

"This is no time for joking, Chuchie! Could you please talk to Esmeralda?"

"Okay, put her on."

I hand the receiver to Esmeralda, and wait with bated breath while the two of them talk in Spanish. Esmeralda hands the phone back to me, and Chanel isn't so chirpy anymore.

"You've got to get your father out of there—he's been hexed!" Chanel says, worried.

"Esmeralda says the place is jinxed by a *bruja*—a witch, and not a good one either. Someone has placed your father under some kind of spell, and those are voodoo dolls on the mantel!"

I hear someone mumbling in the background to Chanel, and she says, "Wait a minute, Aqua!"

I hold on while Chanel talks with someone—probably loverboy Lizard. My hands are freezing, because I'm so scared for Daddy. I knew that High Priestess Abala Shaballa was up to no good! *We have to get Daddy to a hospital!*

"Please, Chanel, hurry up." I peer up at Esmeralda and give her a look, like, "I understand." Her eyes are pleading with me.

"Eddie says don't take your father to a hospital!" Chanel says. "He needs to be looked at by a hoodoo practitioner!" I hear Eddie in the background, still talking to her.

"We are calling 911 as soon we hang up, so an ambulance can take Daddy to a hospital, Chanel," I say firmly. Eddie Lizard may have Galleria and Chanel under a spell with all his hoodoo talk, but he doesn't fool me. "We can't just leave Daddy lying here like this."

"No, no—the doctors can't help!" Chanel says excitedly.

"And I guess Eddie Lizard can?" I shoot back, annoyed.

"No, he'll call his father to come over and look at him," Chanel says.

"Daddy's going to the hospital, and that's that," I huff back.

Suddenly, Eddie Lizard gets on the phone. "Listen, um, Aqua—"

"Aquanette," I repeat, annoyed that he can't even remember my name properly.

"Yes, Aquanette—even if you do take your father to the hospital, don't touch anything in your house. Let my father come over and see what's going on."

"Well, okay—we'll call you as soon as we get back. Bye," I say, anxious to get off the phone.

"Excuse me, Aquanette—but how are you going to call without my father's phone number?"

"Oh. Right—give it to me," I say, embarrassed. I scribble it down on a pad. Then I hang up the phone, and pick it up again to dial 911.

"I don't care what Eddie Lizard says," I hiss to Angie. "Daddy is going to the hospital."

"No hospital!" Esmeralda says, placing my

palm in hers. I wonder why she's hopping on the same hoodoo bandwagon. . . .

"No, no—he's going, and that's final!" I say, determined. Nobody is gonna tell me what to do with my daddy. "And if that 'pecan nut' Abala Shaballa Cuckoo comes around here again, I'm going to hit her over her head with her own broomstick!"

Chapter 6

It seems like we've been waiting for a thousand years in the emergency room at St. Luke's Hospital for someone to come and tell us what's wrong with Daddy. The ambulance workers put him on a stretcher, and he seemed delirious the whole way over, sweating and mumbling.

We'd never ridden in the back of an ambulance before—and if we never do again, it will be too soon. I couldn't help crying, and neither could Angie. We weren't worried about scaring Daddy, because he didn't even seem to know we were there with him. He just kept mumbling strange things, and calling out to that strange woman— "Mattie, is that you? I won't leave you."

"We'd better call Ma later," Angie says, as if she's thinking out loud.

"Suit yourself," I mumble back. "I wonder if she knows who Mattie is. . . ."

"Probably," Angie says, shrugging her shoulders.

By now, I have a pretty good idea of who Mattie must be—some woman Daddy knows from his past. Angie is clutching my hand as we wait in the emergency room, which is scary in itself. As a matter of fact, we feel like we're in a bad version of *Fright of the Living Dead*.

I mean, you have to see these people in the emergency room to believe it! The man in the chair next to us, for example, is wearing a bloody ace bandage around his head, like it's an accessory or something. He keeps jumping up out of his chair and prancing back and forth, as if he's giving a fashion show.

The lady sitting across from us has eyebrows so thick, they look like a unibrow across her forehead. But that's not the worst part—she keeps belching so loud that no one will sit next to her—not even her husband! Yes, ma'am, he is sitting a few seats away with a newspaper covering his face—I guess because he's embarrassed, or else he's very interested in the articles he's reading.

He can't be more embarrassed than we are, because Angie and I won't even look up—just in case we accidentally meet the glances of the Unibrow Belcher or Mr. Bloody Ace Bandage.

See, it's hard to be inconspicuous when you're twins—everyone thinks they can just talk to you out of the blue. People always ask the same question, too—as if their eyes are on vacation. "Are you two identical twins?" Usually we don't mind, but right now, I guess I'm not too happy about being a twin—or sitting here in this awful emergency room.

As if hearing me thinking to myself, the Unibrow lady lets out a loud belch. I act like I don't hear a thing. Just another day sitting in a crazy emergency room. Yes, ma'am. I just keep staring at my sneakers, like I'm gonna discover gold any second now.

"Some people should stop makin' so much noise," says an older woman in a blue house-dress with a purple sweater over it, with a big ol' cast on her left arm.

"I think we should call Galleria and Chanel, and tell them what's going on," Angie suggests calmly.

"You call them," I respond.

"Gimme a quarter," Angie mumbles under her breath. I pretend like I don't hear her.

"Come on Aqua, gimme a quarter!"

I hand my pesty sister a quarter, and watch as she heads to the phone booth to call Galleria and Chanel. I don't know why Angie is bothering. What's Galleria gonna do about about this mess with Daddy—write a song? It's not like she can help or anything.

I get so tired of sitting there waiting that I pull out the newspaper and read my horoscope again: *The unconditional love for which you yearn cannot be bought at any price. . . . Watch out for sheep wearing wolves' clothing. . . .*

I still can't figure out what the first part means, but now I think I understand the second part. All along, I've known that High Priestess Abala Shaballa wasn't exactly Glinda the Good Witch, popping into our lives out of nowhere in her magical bubble. (Actually, Daddy met her at the annual African American Expo at the Jacob Javits Convention Center downtown.) Angie and I have always felt that Abala Shaballa is not what she appears to be!

In the House with Mouse!

Please, God, let Daddy be okay! I pray silently. Suddenly, I get scared that Daddy won't wake up—in more ways than one. What if he thinks we're making up this stuff about Abala? What if he thinks his illness doesn't have anything to do with her and all those hocus-pocus brews she's been making him drink?

Suddenly, I get a chill down my spine. What if his illness *doesn't* have anything to do with High Priestess Abala? After all, Esmeralda is Mrs. Elliot's housekeeper—not the Wizard of Oz. How would she know about all that stuff in Daddy's bedroom?

Just then, Angie comes back and plops back into the chair beside me. "Galleria, Chanel, and Eddie want to come over to our house and look at the stuff in Daddy's bedroom," she whispers. "They want to bring Eddie's father, too— Doktor Lizard."

"Well, I don't know if we should be inviting company over to our apartment without Daddy's permission," I shoot back.

Angie gives me a look, like, "You've got to be kidding."

"I don't believe in all this mess anyway," I continue.

Now my sister throws me that look again, and rolls her neck at the same time, which really gets on my nerves.

"Well, never mind what *I* believe in—let's just hear what the doctor has to say," I say, holding my ground. Right now, I don't feel like a Cheetah Girl at all—just a stubborn mule digging its heels in for the long haul.

"Well, I told them we're gonna call them back. I knew you would get mad if they met us at the hospital," Angie says, sucking her teeth.

"Why would you want them coming to the hospital?" I ask her. My sister just doesn't use her head sometimes. I could swear *she's* the one with a crush on Eddie Lizard. "I don't know why you're in such a hurry to have some snake doctor nosing around our house!"

"He's not a snake doctor, he's a hoodoo practitioner!" Angie says, like Miss Smarty Britches.

Luckily, just then a nurse attendant comes out of one of the examining rooms and motions to us. We jump up, following the nurse into a little waiting room.

"Your father is resting. The doctor will be in to see you shortly," she says, smiling. I try to read whatever I can into the nurse's smile, but she just leaves us sitting there. It seems like a thousand more hours before a tall doctor wearing glasses comes in to talk to us. "Is there a Mrs. Walker?"

"No—um, yes, sir, but our mother lives in Houston," I say, suddenly feeling embarrassed that Daddy is lying in some room and Ma isn't here with us.

"Okay, well, your father is going to be fine," the doctor continues. "He's quite dehydrated, and his blood pressure is low, but after a series of tests, we can't find any medical reason to detain him further. We'll release him in the morning, after we run a few more tests."

"There isn't anything wrong with him?" I ask, surprised. How can that be? I just *knew* the doctor was going to tell us something horrible. I feel the sweat breaking out on my forehead.

"Like I said—he's severely dehydrated, but we can't detect any other underlying medical conditions. His vitals are all relatively stable," the doctor says, poker-faced.

I don't care what he says—I *know* there is something wrong with our Daddy.

"Can you arrange for someone—an adult—

to come tomorrow, so we release your father in the morning?" the doctor asks.

"Yes, sir, we'll come with an adult in the morning," I say, snapping out of my daze.

As we leave the hospital, Angie looks at me and doesn't say a word. I don't want to admit it, but for once, I think she is right. I turn to her, tears welling in my eyes, and mumble, "We'd better have Doktor Snake make a house call."

Angie just holds me, and doesn't say a word, which is a blessing. Even though I always gloat about being three minutes older, for once I feel like *I'm* the younger twin.

Chapter 7

When we get back home, we both feel scared about going upstairs by ourselves.

"Let's go get Esmeralda!" Angie says.

"We've scared that poor woman enough for one day," I mutter. "We'd better be glad Esmeralda doesn't speak English so she can't tell Mrs. Elliot about the afternoon 'fright' we gave her—and all the strange things she saw in Daddy's bedroom."

"Yes, ma'am!" Angie replies knowingly.

That's all we would need, is for all our neighbors in the building to think they have a bunch of "pecan nuts" from Houston living next door to them!

Taking a deep breath, we climb the spiral

staircase. Scaredy-cat or not, I think it's high time we figure out what on earth all those strange things are in Daddy's bedroom.

"We left the light on," I say out loud, as if Daddy is still home. Even now, I can hear his voice fussing with us about that. He is real particular about us turning off all the lights, so we don't "give his money away to Con Edison."

"I didn't leave it on," Angie says, defending herself as usual.

"It doesn't matter who left it on," I shoot back, "'cuz Daddy's in the hospital." I can't even remember who left the room last after the EMS (Emergency Medical Service) workers got Daddy in the ambulance. The first thing I do is go straight for the mess on the nightstand.

"Somebody musta put all this stuff in Daddy's room after we went to Drinka Champagne's," Angie says, like she's honing her divette detective skills. I think she'd better stick to her neurosurgeon ambitions, because I am definitely better at clues than she is.

"What do you mean, *somebody*?" I huff back. "It's *obvious* who."

"Well, why would Abala do this?" Angie

says, peering at Daddy's nightstand and reaching for something.

"Now that's a dim-witted remark, Angie," I say, shaking my head at her.

She ignores me. Picking up one of the voodoo dolls, she starts shaking it.

"Don't touch anything until Doktor Lizard gets here!" I yell at her like I'm the chief investigating officer on this crime scene.

"I thought you didn't believe in any of this stuff," Angie challenges me, smirking like the Cheshire Cat.

"I don't," I say, realizing that I'm acting stubborn again. Well, I can't help it! Like Big Momma says, *A scorpion can't change its ways, so why should people?*

"I've never seen black candles before," Angie says, leaning over and looking at the burned votive candles. "I wonder what those are for?"

I stare at all the other stuff on the nightstand. Aside from the black and red candles and the funny-looking brown-cloth dolls, there are stones, powders, herbs, an old-fashioned scale, some nails, and a little sack.

"It looks like she burned something else besides the candles," I say, surprised by the pile of ashes on the nightstand. "It kinda looks like photos—people's pictures, maybe?"

Angie examines the pile of ashes. "Those are definitely the edges of photos, and magazine pages."

"Yeah, you're right—magazine pages. I didn't think of that," I say.

The doorbell rings, and we both jump.

"That must be Galleria and the snake people!" Angie says, like a smart-aleck. I know she's making fun of me.

When we open the door and see Galleria's face, I forget how I upset I got at her earlier. That is, until Eddie Lizard appears in the doorway, flashing his devilishly charming smile. That familiar voice I heard in my head all morning pays me another visit. *Why does he have to like Galleria? Why can't he like me?*

"Where's Chanel and Dorinda?" Angie asks Galleria.

"Auntie Juanita would have a fit if Chanel stayed out any longer. We put her in a cab. She's not supposed to be hopping around all day on those crutches. Miss Cuchifrita Ballerina is still a crippled Cheetah, you know." Galleria looks at me like she wants to make peace. "And you know, Dorinda has to help out Mrs. Bosco on Saturdays with cleaning."

"I know that's right," I say, catching my manners and trying not to act jealous again. Now I just feel disappointed. We've gotten used to Chanel and Dorinda being involved in everything we do, so it only seems right that they should be here with us now.

"Hi, um, Aquanette," Eddie says, trying to be polite. I look at him, and feel my heart fluttering. Then he steps aside and an older man comes into the apartment after him. Eddie's father looks just like him—except that he's older, taller, and has white hair. I know I should tell Eddie he looks just like his father, but I don't want to.

Judging from Doktor Lizard's white gauze outfit and moccasins, I can tell he's not from New York, and that he's used to living in a warmer climate. I look down at his moccasins again—the toes are pointy like Aladdin's slippers. Jack Frost must be nipping at his heels quite a bit. "I'm sorry, sir, but I'm Aquanette Walker, and this is my sister Anginette," I say, catching my manners and holding out my hand to shake his.

The peaceful-looking man covers my hand with both of his, and stands still for a second—so I don't move either. Slowly, he removes his hands, then says, "I'm Doktor Lizard—Eddie's father."

Doktor Lizard does the same exact thing to Angie. As we all walk into the living room, Galleria whispers in my ear, "He's just trying to feel your vibrations." Then she pinches my butt, which causes me to giggle.

Doktor Lizard turns in front of the couch and smiles. "Let's go see the handiwork."

"Excuse me?" I ask, feeling stupid because I don't know what he's talking about.

"Upstairs," Galleria whispers, nudging my back.

"Oh, yes. Can we get you any lemonade or something to drink first?" Angie asks.

"No, thanks—I've imbibed quite a bit already," Doktor Lizard says, smiling.

Imbibe? Lord, that's just what we need—someone else talking funny. It sure seems like we can't understand what anybody is trying to tell us today!

"This is definitely the work of a spooky kook," Galleria says, sniffing the burnt air in Daddy's bedroom.

"No. This is the work of someone who has made a pact with the devil," Doktor Lizard says, "to try and win the love of a man forever, so she can control him." He moves closer, to see the stuff on the nightstand.

I can tell by how slowly and carefully Doktor Lizard is talking that he's trying not to frighten us. Well, it isn't working—I look over at Angie, and I can tell he is scaring both of us to death!

"She burned photos—probably of women—desirable women . . . women he used to love," Doktor Lizard explains.

"Why?"

"To eliminate the competition, and to insure that he will love no other, nor harbor any lingering flames." Doktor Lizard nods knowingly. "This sort of ritual is only performed by Hexagone witches."

"Our Daddy's girlfriend's name is Abala Shaballa Hexagone!" I blurt out.

"Oh, well, then there is no mystery about what is going on here," Doktor Lizard says, picking up the pouch on the nightstand and emptying the stuff inside.

I try to peer over his shoulder and see without being rude, but I don't know what those things are he's holding in his hands.

"My, my, my—I haven't seen the likes of these in centuries," Doktor Lizard says, looking at us and smiling.

Centuries? I hope he's joking, because he can't be that old!

"A piece of elephant tusk, an alligator tooth, and the bill of a mockingbird in a bogo mojo bag." Doktor Lizard toys with the items in his hand, like he's marveling at Abala's "handiwork."

"It's all here," he says. "She's created an altar for the spell—black candles to signify the negative forces inherent within the multiverse. Red candles to incite passion. Voodoo dolls stuffed with straw, his bodily fluids, nail clippings, and clothing."

I grab Angie's hand and clutch it tight. I never believed that anything could scare us more than the horror movies we love to watch—but Doktor Lizard has succeeded!

"Stones to set the time of their romance to infinity. Nails to write the spell on the candles," Doktor Lizard continues, like he's doing his grocery list. "Scales to weigh out his love, and the exact quantities of the herbs, roots, and powders for her potions."

"She's been making him drink brews for weeks now!" I blurt out. "She tried to get *us* to drink them too."

"Yes, well, she wouldn't have gone to this extreme unless something was going wrong," Doktor Lizard says, resting his finger on his lips. "She must have discovered that his heart belonged to someone else."

Suddenly, my heart stops—maybe Daddy really *does* still love Ma! "Well, it would have to be our mother—she lives in Houston," I explain quickly.

"I see," Doktor Lizard says, while taking out a bag from his leather satchel.

"I must uncross the spell here first."

"How do you do that?" Galleria asks.

"Uncrossing oil, jinx removal, and hocus-pocus powder," Doktor Lizard says nonchalantly. He opens a bottle and sprinkles drops everywhere, while chanting: "Break the hex, blast the root, free this man from the Hexagone hoot!"

Galleria takes her Kitty Kat notebook from her backpack. *I can't believe she's gonna write this stuff down!* It figures Galleria would try to make a song out of anything—even Daddy's misery! I cut my eyes at Angie, who just shrugs.

"Now we must go examine the crossroads," Doktor Lizard mumbles, like he's talking to himself.

"What crossroads?"

"When you walk to the corner, there's a pole, and when you look up, you see the sign for the street and the avenue, pointing in two different directions," Eddie explains for his father.

"The intersection of two roads, two street signs, is a place of great magical power. It's also the best place to dispose of the remnants of a spell—leftover candle wax, incense and photo ashes, footprint dirt, ground bone fragments," Doktor Lizard says, gathering the stuff off the nightstand and putting it carefully in his bag.

"Do you want us to help you?" I ask.

"We're losing light, so we have to hurry," Eddie Lizard says quickly. "Later, you and your sister should clean the room as well as you can—before your father comes home from the hospital."

"Oh, okay," I say, trying not to look at him while he talks. I know this is silly, but Eddie Lizard just makes me feel so self-conscious. I cut a quick glance at Galleria. I can tell she is truly smitten with him.

"We have to go remove the remnants, then visit the hospital and attend to your father," Doktor Lizard calmly explains. "With all their medical expertise, doctors are never able to detect the work of a spell, hex, curse, or devil's pact."

"Can we help Daddy?" I ask hopefully.

"Well, the sun hasn't gone down yet, so we still have some time. I will do my best," Doktor Lizard says, kissing the talisman charm around his neck.

When we get to the corner of Eighty-ninth Street and Riverside Drive, Doktor Lizard instructs us to go through every piece of garbage. I feel so funny, because people are staring at us. They probably think we are homeless people—or even worse, that we're up to no good.

"That's mine!" screams a homeless woman who has appeared out of nowhere. She has bright red lipstick smeared across her mouth. "Don't touch my stuff!" she yells, lunging at me so quickly that I drop the empty milk carton I'm holding.

"This is hoodoo business, woman—scat!" Doktor Lizard says without moving a muscle. The lady gets a scared look on her face and walks off, babbling.

How did he do that? I wonder.

"The power of hoodoo is known by many," Doktor Lizard says, as if reading my mind.

Well, we sure didn't know anything about hoodoo. Not that I'm convinced that all this poking around in public garbage cans is gonna make Daddy better!

"Well, our work is done here," Doktor Lizard announces, after he quietly puts more stuff into his satchel.

"I'm real glad you came," I whisper to Galleria as we get into Doktor Lizard's blue Cadillac and head over to the hospital. When we arrive and announce that we want to see Mr. Walker, the nurse attendant looks at us rather skeptically, but she lets us go up to Daddy's room.

"What are you gonna tell your mother?" Galleria asks me as we walk down the long corridor. Galleria knows, because she stayed at our mother's house in Houston with us, that Angie and I haven't told our mother bo-peep about High Priestess Abala Shaballa. How are we supposed to tell Ma the truth *now*, after we've been fibbing all this time? *The Lord doesn't like liars*, I can hear Ma's voice ringing in my ear.

"She's gonna be so hurt that we lied to her about what was going on with Daddy and that pecan nut!" I whisper to Galleria. "We're gonna have to tell her the truth—eventually."

"She may try to take you back from your father," Galleria says nervously. "What if she wants you and Angie to move back to Houston?"

I know what Galleria is getting at. We *can't* move back to Houston and leave the Cheetah Girls behind!

"Daddy looks so peaceful," Angie sighs as we gather around his bed.

The nurse from the desk comes inside and tells us, "He's resting now, so we're gonna have to ask you to leave."

"Oh, please, ma'am—I just need to look at my father for comfort. We won't disturb a thing," I plead with her.

The nurse looks at Doktor Lizard like she's unsure what to do. "All right," she finally says.

When she leaves, I crack a smile.

"That was quite a performance—you drama queen!" Galleria whispers, complimenting me on my theatrics. I guess I have learned a thing or two, going to LaGuardia Performing Arts

Annex with a whole bunch of real-life drama queens.

Doktor Lizard reaches over the hospital bed and tries to open Daddy's eyelids. Then he touches his palms, heart, and head. "I'm gonna need your help," he says, motioning for us to help prop Daddy up in his bed.

"Anginette, go guard the door to make sure the nurse doesn't come in," Doktor Lizard commands my sister.

When we've propped Daddy up, Eddie Lizard holds him still while his father prepares something in a bowl. "This is a 'decoction'— the opposite of a concoction—it should help undo the Love Spell."

Daddy doesn't even open his eyes as we open his mouth and hold the cup to it so he can gulp down the decoction.

"She almost had him, that's for sure," Doktor Lizard comments, as he pulls out a piece of paper and a fancy-looking pen. "I'm writing your father's name on parchment paper with dragon's blood ink, to help him heal," Doktor Lizard says, looking at me until I realize he's waiting for me to tell him Daddy's name.

"Oh, I'm sorry—his name is John Walker."

After Doktor Lizard finishes writing Daddy's name, he puts the paper on the nightstand, takes out two white candles from a case, and lights them on the table. Then he places some oil on one of the voodoo dolls, and puts it on Daddy's chest. "I'm going to recite an incantation to gain the help of the healing spirits," Doktor Lizard explains. "You won't be able to understand my chant as I drift into the unknown tongue, but do not be frightened."

Galleria nods her head, and I grab her hand as we listen to Doktor Lizard making funny noises and words. *"Abba—hum, dweebie dum, raccaacaacaa, dummmmmmmm."*

It just sounds like Doktor Lizard is calling somebody dumb, but I have no idea what he's really saying. Angie turns around, startled, but I motion for her to keep guarding the door. After Doktor Lizard finishes his chant, he wraps the voodoo doll and parchment paper in a piece of white cloth and places it between the two white candles.

All of a sudden, the patient in the bed next to Daddy's turns over and yells out, "Hey, if it isn't the Bobbsey Twins!"

My heart almost jumps out of my chest, until

I realize that it's Mr. Bloody Ace Bandage from the emergency room. "That's right, it's us," I whisper to him. "Shhh, we don't want to wake our Daddy!"

"Oh, okay," the man says, then turns back over.

"Don't worry, we're finished here," Doktor Lizard assures me as he packs up everything.

"Who was that wack attack?" Galleria asks, puzzled, as we flee Daddy's hospital room. "The Bobbsey Twins—funny we never thought of calling you that."

"Well, you thought of everything else to call us," I reply sarcastically, then wrap my arm under Galleria's. I'm not mad at her—I'm just anxious to find out if Doktor Lizard's ritual worked.

As if reading my mind, Doktor Lizard calmly tells us, "Now all we have to do is wait and see. You'll have to watch your father's behavior closely when he's released."

"Don't worry, we'll watch him like Houston hawks!"

"What do we do about Abala?" Angie asks, like a scaredy-cat.

"Nothing," Doktor Lizard says. "She'll know that she's failed—that he doesn't love her—and she'll find another victim."

I feel a pang in my chest, as if Doktor Lizard is talking about *me*. He probably knows a lot more about people's secrets than he's telling. He probably already knows that I like his son, and that Eddie doesn't like me.

I sit quietly in the back of the car with Galleria and Angie, while Eddie Lizard sits up front with his father. My nosy sister whispers something in Galleria's ear. Galleria whispers back, loud enough for me to hear: "No, silly willy—I'm just mackin'."

Now I know what Angie asked her—if she liked Eddie.

Suddenly, I realize what the first part of my horoscope meant—you can't make someone like you. They either like you or they don't. Well, I don't care anymore if Galleria does like Eddie, or if he likes her. They deserve each other!

Chapter 8

The next morning, Angie and I come straight home after church to call the hospital, and see if Daddy can be released.

"Yes, Mr. Walker is being discharged today," an attendant tells us over the phone.

"Really?" I ask, like I can't believe it.

"Yes, the residing doctor has ordered his discharge. Everything seems to be fine. He'll need an adult to sign him out."

"Yes, we know," I reply.

"We can pick up Daddy!" I shout to Angie, who throws her arms around my neck and hugs me, stepping on my nicely shined pumps in the process.

"Ouch, Angie—you're gonna put *me* in the hospital now!" I say.

But she just slaps me on the shoulder and smiles. "'Member how Uncle Skeeter told us that when he was younger, Big Momma used to pay him five dollars to walk around in her shoes to stretch them out?"

"Yeah—no wonder he can't keep his head on straight!" I chuckle back. "Dag on, I wish Uncle Skeeter was here right now. I could use some cheerin' up."

"Me, too," Angie mumbles.

We'd never realized until this morning—when we tried to think of an adult to bring along to check Daddy out of the hospital—how *sad* we felt about not having any relatives in New York. You have to understand, we have so many relatives spread all over down South, that when we have our annual family reunion picnic in Bayou Wildlife Park, we take up the whole eighty-six acres! Okay, maybe I'm exaggerating just a bit, but we have more relatives than most people.

"It's just plain pitiful that we had to ask Ms. Dorothea and Mr. Garibaldi to take us to St. Luke's and sign Daddy out," I say, shaking my head. We didn't know who else to ask—and believe me, it kills us to have to ask Galleria for anything, after yesterday's drama.

I know we could have asked somebody at our church—Hallelujah Tabernacle—but we don't know the people in our congregation that well. Besides, Reverend Butter, and the pastors and aides, are real busy getting everything ready for our big Christmas celebration—that's all everybody over there is talking about.

"I hope Daddy doesn't act strange in front of Ms. Dorothea," Angie mutters while we change the sheets on his bed—just like Docktor Lizard and his son Eddie suggested we do. (Of course, Angie and I were too tired to finish cleaning last night, because Galleria kept the Cheetah Girls in the chat room, swooning about Eddie Lizard, till I was bitten to death by the green-eyed monster!)

I drill Angie on how we're gonna play it with Mr. and Mrs. Garibaldi. "As far as Bubbles's parents are concerned, Daddy fell faint from dehydration and stress, and had to go the hospital for some tests. After all, they know how hard Daddy's been working at his new job at SWAT Bug Spray, whipping up marketing campaigns for the new flea spray they're launching in the spring."

We've already asked the Lord to forgive us for "withholding information"—that's what Big Momma calls it when you don't tell people the whole truth about something until the right moment.

"Should we call Ma now and tell her?" Angie asks.

"And tell her what?" I counter. "If you ask me, I'd rather wait until the sun goes down on this mess."

"But we always call her or Big Momma after church on Sundays!" Angie protests.

"Well, we're busy living our lives in the Big Apple, so I'm sure they'll understand if we call later," I snap back at her. Shoot, I may be stubborn as a mule, but Angie just plain kicks stuff around like a mindless donkey!

The doorbell rings, and I run to the door with my coat in my hand, because I know it's Mr. Garibaldi and Ms. Dorothea. Now Angie will have to move her slowpoke butt away from the telephone, and stop thinking about calling Ma or Big Momma and broadcasting Daddy's problems all over the country!

"Hi, Aquanetta!" Mr. Garibaldi exclaims, kissing me on both cheeks. I just love when he does that! (It's a European salutation, I guess.)

"Hello, Miz Aqua," Galleria says, squinting at me to keep the sun out of her eyes. If I didn't know better, I would swear Galleria is acting insecure.

"Where's Angie? Let's get this rodeo on the road," Ms. Dorothea says, clutching the collar on her fake cheetah-fur coat.

"Angie! Let's go," I yell loudly.

She finally comes downstairs, and we run outside to Mr. Garibaldi's van. "What station do you girls want to hear?" he asks once we get comfy inside.

"Hot 99, Daddy—we've gotta hear the new jammies!" Galleria blurts out, speaking for all of us as usual.

"So, what new songs are you girls working on?" Mr. Garibaldi asks excitedly. I wonder why he asks *us* that. He should be asking his daughter, since she's the one who writes all our songs.

"Um . . ." I start in, but Galleria cuts me off.

"Daddy, you know we aren't working on anything until Chanel gets better, or until we hear from the Def Duck peeps about a showcase, or getting in the studio with Mouse Almighty!"

"That's quite an earful, darling. I hope you spurt out sound bytes for interviews as quick as you spurt out your *whines*," Ms. Dorothea comments, like she's a reporter doing commentary.

"I wasn't whining, I was just saying," Galleria replies with a smirk.

The new song "Hot Diggity Dog," by Kenny Knuckles, comes on the radio, and the three of us sing along, because we know all the words:

"You can pay your rent
So you think you're heaven sent
Don't wreck my life and cause me strife
'Cuz I'm going for mine all the time
Hot Diggity Dog
Don't mean I'm the alley cat with a wack attack
Hot Diggity Dog
Don't mean I can't be down with the mack
Hot Diggity to my Dogs
Then we can all get along in this song!"

"You think they play this song enough? That's the thirtieth time this morning, and we haven't even had our breakfast yet!" Ms. Dorothea moans.

"You know how it is when a new jammy comes out, they give it major-domo airtime," Galleria says, bopping along.

"Who's the artist?" Ms. Dorothea asks. She's real interested in the new acts coming up, now that she is officially our manager.

"Kenny Knuckles," I reply.

"Kenny 'Pig' Knuckles is more like it— 'cuz he's packing an extra fifty in the music video for the single," Galleria snorts.

Suddenly I feel uncomfortable. Angie and I aren't exactly fluttering doves in the weight department. Maybe, when the Cheetah Girls start getting famous, people will say the same thing about us!

"You know, you always look heavier on television than in person," I retort, crouching a little farther back into my seat so I don't take up so much room. "It's not fair that male artists can be as big as the post office, but nobody says anything. I don't like the fact that people expect female artists to be skinny, like Mariah, Kahlua, or Whitney—it just isn't right." I fall silent, hoping Ms. Dorothea will come to our defense.

"In my opinion, as long as you don't eat all the

profits from the record trough, you're entitled to a few good meals," Ms. Dorothea quips, coming through for me. But then, she asks the question I was hoping wouldn't come up this morning. "Aqua, what exactly happened yesterday?"

I get a queasy feeling in my stomach. I wonder if Galleria told her mother about Eddie Lizard. She probably even told her that I liked him!

"W-what do you mean?" I respond, stuttering.

"When you came home from vocal practice?" Ms. Dorothea asks suspiciously.

"Oh, we, um, Daddy was lying in bed, and said he didn't feel too good," I say, cutting my eyes at Angie, who throws me a glance faster than greased lightning.

"That's all?" Ms. Dorothea asks, like she doesn't believe us.

"Yes, ma'am."

"Don't you think it's odd that a grown man wouldn't have called the hospital himself?" Dorothea continues interrogating me.

"Um, yes, but I think he was waiting for us," Angie mumbles, so low that Ms. Dorothea asks her to repeat herself.

Ms. Dorothea doesn't ask us any more questions, though. I'm so glad when we finally get to the hospital, I almost jump out of the car before Mr. Garibaldi puts his foot on the brakes!

I know Ms. Dorothea doesn't believe us, but right now the only thing I care about is getting Daddy out of this place, and seeing if the spell has really been broken.

"Daddy!" Angie says excitedly when she sees our father sitting quietly in the outpatient room. Daddy stares back at us sternly, which causes my heart to flutter. I think Daddy really has recovered, and is back to his old self. Well, praise the Lord and shame that headwrap-wearing "She-devil!"

"Mr. Walker," Mr. Garibaldi starts in, putting his arm around Daddy's shoulder.

"Call me John," Daddy says politely.

"*Sí, sí*—forgive me, *Giovanni*!" Mr. Garibaldi says, grinning from ear to ear.

"I like the way your name sounds in Italian, Daddy," I say, smiling.

Daddy doesn't say a word, but Mr. Garibaldi just keeps chattering away. "Can we expect you at our dinner table at eight o'clock? The lobster fra diavolo is simmering *perfetto* right now, and waiting for you later!"

"Of course, I don't see why not—eight

o'clock, as planned," Daddy chuckles. Mr. Garibaldi could make dead people smile in their coffins if he wanted to.

"Mr. Garibaldi, what does lobster fra . . . um, you know, mean?" I ask, grinning because I cannot pronounce the word. (I'm sorry—I'm just terrible at trying to say things in other languages.)

"Lobster fra diavolo?" Mr. Garibaldi repeats, humoring me.

"Yes, sir," I shoot back.

"It means, lobster à la Friar Devil," Mr. Garibaldi explains.

My heart stops right in its tracks. *No, please, not the devil again!* Mr. Garibaldi sees the shocked look on my face, and quickly goes on to explain. "No, *cara*, it does not mean that exactly—um, how do you say—?"

"It's not a literal translation," Galleria says, throwing a smirk in my direction.

Since she knows the truth about Daddy, I guess she's entitled to get a good laugh from that one. "It's just a fancy way of saying spicy spaghetti with some seafood thrown in the mix—definitely the flavor that you two savor."

I feel a sting in my chest when Galleria says

that—and she catches it too, by the look on my face. Suddenly, I feel stupid, because I realize Galleria doesn't mean anything bad by those things she says. I'm just being overly sensitive. Shoot, before that cute boy in a snakeskin rattled his way into Drinka Champagne's, I would have paid Galleria's remarks no mind—as a matter of fact, Angie and I laugh at her jokes all the time.

"Aquanetta, you havva not lost faith in my cooking, no?" Mr. Garibaldi says, teasing me.

"Oh, no, Mr. Garibaldi, we will be at your table at eight o'clock sharp!" I reply quickly. "Dorinda and Chanel are coming too, right?"

"Yes, ma'am," Galleria says, imitating me, then putting her arm around my shoulder. "Don't forget to tell me my horror-scope later!"

I feel myself cringing *again* at Galleria's remark, but this time I stop myself. Galleria always asks me to read her "horror-scope," because she gets a kick out of it. Being the capricious Gemini she is, she's always full of tricks and surprises!

"See you later, Ms. Dorothea."

"Bye, darlings—be on time, and don't wear

white!" she quips, making a joke about the hospital uniforms, I guess.

The first thing we do when we get back inside our house is walk over to the ugly Bogo Mogo Hexagone Warrior Mask, turn to Daddy, and ask, "Is it okay if we take this thing down now?"

"Throw it out—I don't want to ever see that thing again!" Looking defeated, Daddy walks upstairs to his bedroom.

"Good-bye, Bogo," Angie mutters, as we stuff it into the trash can outside the building.

"I don't trust this thing—why don't we throw it in the garbage down the block?" I say, pulling it back out. We know we're not supposed to do that, because people are real fussy about their garbage cans in New York. One day, I saw Mrs. Elliot yelling at the people in the building next door, because they left a stack of magazines for recycling in front of our building.

"Yeah, let's put Mr. Bogo in a garbage bin far away from us!" Angie quips.

After we say good-bye to Mr. Bogo for the last time (we hope), we go straight back up to Daddy's bedroom to see if he's okay.

"How are you feelin', Daddy?" I ask. But he just sits on the edge of his bed like a robot. We sit next to him quietly, until the spirit moves me to tell him exactly what my horoscope said yesterday.

"The unconditional love for which you yearn cannot be bought at any price."

All of a sudden, Daddy puts his head down in his hands, and starts bawling like a baby! I have never seen Daddy cry like this, except for the day our parents' divorce papers came through. He sat at the dining room table that day, looked at the papers for the longest time, then cried.

"It's been so lonely up here without your mother," Daddy blurts out all of a sudden.

"We know, Daddy," Angie pipes up. "We didn't tell you, but you should have seen how lonely Ma is down there without you."

Daddy gets real quiet for a long time, then whispers, "There wasn't anything wrong with me a doctor could fix, was there?"

"No, Daddy, there wasn't," I reply calmly. "Do you remember us coming to the hospital yesterday with, um, Doktor Lizard, and his son?"

"No," Daddy says. "The last thing I remember is Abala coming over after you girls left for your vocal lessons."

"Daddy, who is Mattie?" I blurt out.

From the look on Daddy's face, I know I have stepped on a land mine. Angie gets real still.

"Why do you ask?" he asks, looking guilty.

"Because you mumbled her name when you were sleeping." I hold my breath, waiting for Daddy to answer.

"I was with her . . . before your mother," Daddy says solemnly.

Now I wish Daddy hadn't told me who Mattie was. Then I wouldn't know that he still loves her. I can tell he does by the look in his eyes.

"I told Abala that I still carried a torch for Mattie," Daddy confesses. "I mean, she was my first real love. I think that's normal, but I don't think Abala took it the right way."

"Maybe that's why she sped up the spell!" Angie says, playing divette detective again.

"Did you tell her anything about Ma?" I ask hopefully.

"Yes, I did—I told her that I still love your mother . . . very much," Daddy says, putting his hands to his face.

"Well, it sounds like Abala might have pan-icked, and tried to erase all the memories from your heart," I say, thinking out loud.

"Anything else?" Daddy asks sternly, looking at me and Angie, like, "The True Confessions Show is over, and stay tuned for the next episode!"

"Um, no, Daddy—we just wanted to make sure you're okay," I say, heaving a deep sigh. Daddy has had enough drama this weekend to last until—well, until Ma calls, anyway.

"I feel fine," he says, still threatening us with his eyes. "And don't you girls have homework to do?"

"Yes, we do!" Angie and I say in unison, smiling with relief. We turn to go, but Daddy stops us.

"Tell me one thing—" he says.

"Yes, Daddy?" I hold my breath. *Please, God, don't let him know that I had a crush on Eddie Lizard. I hope he hasn't figured that out!*

"You didn't tell your mother I was in the hospital, did you?"

"No, Daddy, we didn't," I say softly.

"Good. Please don't say anything—yet," he says firmly.

"Okay," I say, relieved that Daddy doesn't know anything about Eddie Lizard. Daddy doesn't take kindly to us liking boys, I don't care *what* spell he is under! Like I said, he doesn't want us dating until we're sixteen, and that's that.

"Um, Daddy—you just have to promise us one thing," I tell him.

"I can't promise till I know what it is!" Daddy barks, just like he used to before all this happened. "Come on, out with it!"

"Please don't bring any more of those nasty shakes in this house!" (I'm talking about all those herbs he drank, instead of good meals like we're used to cooking—and Daddy is used to *eating*!)

"That's a promise," Daddy says, breaking out into a small smile, which on him looks bigger than the one on the Cheshire Cat.

We both kiss Daddy on his forehead and run off to our room. "You're gonna help me with my math homework, right?" Angie starts in.

"All right, Miss Smarty-Britches—but you owe me one!" I am determined to make my sister pay for all those snide comments she made yesterday. "And I do not like Eddie Lizard one bit!" I hiss, as she lies on her bed and opens her math notebook.

"I *know* you do!" Angie shoots back, smirking at me.

"It's a long time till sundown, sister, so you'd better pray you don't end up tied to some voodoo doll that looks like a crawling Lizard," I warn her.

"That's right," she says, "'cuz you'll just untie me and tie yourself to it!"

Angie screams as I wrestle her to the floor.

"I thought you girls were doing your homework," Daddy yells from his bedroom.

For the first time, we're dee-lirious that Daddy is yelling at us about something, 'cuz we know he's back to his good old gruffy self again!

Chapter 9

J ust as we're all leaving our apartment to go to Ms. Dorothea's for dinner, the phone rings. It's probably Ma, I think to myself. She must be crawling with crickets because we didn't call her today!

Angie rushes to answer the phone, but I wrestle it from her. I'm sorry, but I still don't trust Angie to talk to Ma yet. She might tell her about what happened, even though Daddy said not to.

"Hello?" The blood drains from my face like a vampire when I hear the voice of High Priestess Abala Shaballa, the woman who hurt our Daddy in the name of love.

"Daddy doesn't want to speak to you anymore, so please don't call our house," I mutter into the phone. I know Daddy can't hear me, because he went to get his Cadillac out of the garage, but I still feel nervous about messing in grown-ups' business.

The High Priestess starts talking, in that breathy voice of hers that makes her sound supernatural. "Well, I do declare, um—"

"It's Aquanette," I say politely

"Well, Aquanette, perhaps you'd better let me speak to your father. I can see you don't understand—"

"Oh, yes, ma'am, we understand all right. As a matter of fact, we *over*stand, because we don't take too kindly to you putting a stupid love spell on our father. He's *through* with you and your brews," I shout. "So go park your broomstick somewhere else! Good-bye!"

"I see," Abala says, like she's embarrassed. "You're quite mistaken, but perhaps I'll call—"

"No, *you* don't understand," I huff, "if you call here again, we're reporting you to the FBI, the CIA, and UFO headquarters!"

"UFO?" Abala repeats, balking.

"Yes, ma'am—because you're definitely from

another planet! Personally, we suggest that you go back to Hexagonia for a brush-up course, 'cuz your witchcraft skills *stink*!"

High Priestess Abala Shaballa hangs up in my ear.

"You think she'll call back here?" Angie asks as we walk to Daddy's car.

"I don't think so," I answer firmly. "She has definitely flown the coop!"

By the time we get to Galleria's apartment on the Upper East Side, we have forgotten all about High Priestess Abala—and I *hope* she has forgotten about *us*! We're excited, because this is the first time we're having dinner at the Garibaldis'. I plan on having a good time, and maybe even being nice to Miss Galleria after yesterday's drama.

"You're not still mad at Galleria, are you?" pesty Angie asks me as Daddy's parking the car near Galleria's apartment building on Sixty-seventh Street.

"She can have Eddie Lizard if she wants," I say, acting nonchalant. "He's too skinny for me anyway."

Angie chuckles her silly little laugh, and

leaves me alone. I swear, she has a mind like a meat cleaver!

"Wazzup, buttercup?" Galleria says, when she opens the door and sees me and Angie. I feel myself cringe inside. Is this another one of Galleria's Southern slanders? She probably thinks we make butter out of buttercup flowers in our backyard!

"Hi, Galleria," Angie says, giving her a kiss on both cheeks the way Mr. Garibaldi does it. Galleria giggles, and does it to me. I kiss her back—on both cheeks—because I know I'm being ree-diculous.

Mr. Garibaldi's face lights up like a Christmas tree when he sees us. "I'm so happy to see my *caras* again—especially sitting at my dinner table," Mr. Garibaldi says, kissing us both twice on each cheek, which causes us to giggle again. "And how are you feeling, Mr. Walker?"

Daddy clears his throat and nods his head, saying, "Fine, fine." I think Daddy must be embarrassed that Mr. Garibaldi picked him up from the hospital—even though we've assured him that we didn't tell Ms. Dorothea or Mr. Garibaldi one bo-peep about his love spell, or uncrossing the hex.

In the House with Mouse!

It's funny, but in the four months we've known her, we've never been in Galleria's apartment before—we always hang out down at Ms. Dorothea's store, Toto in New York—or at Chanel's mom's loft, which has its own dance studio. The Garibaldis' place is just like I imagined it—the most beautiful animal kingdom in the world. "Oh, this is real nice," I tell her quietly as I look around.

"Ooo, look, even the candles are cheetah!" Angie exclaims, pointing at the huge cheetah wax candles in their cheetah candlestick holders.

Galleria's face lights up, like she just got an idea. "*Wazzup, buttercup*—that could be a line in the new song I'm writing!" She picks up her Kitty Kat notebook and plops down on the couch, scribbling away. Dorinda and Chanel are sitting on the couch, too—playing Scrabble.

"Don't get up!" I shout at Chanel. She breaks into a big grin. "It sure doesn't take much for you to start hopping around—and we don't want that!" Then I turn to Dorinda.

"Dorinda, where is your, um, family?" I ask, surprised when I see that she is by herself.

"Mrs. Bosco called and said she'll bring the kids another time. She wanted me to spend time alone with my crew," Dorinda says, breaking into a grin. I can sure tell that she's relieved she isn't "baby-sitting" tonight. "We got the Mariah photos," she adds proudly, pulling out the Cheetah Girls scrapbook that she has started for us.

"Oooh, she looks beautiful even in the photo," I gasp, as I look at the picture of us with Mariah Carey in her dressing room.

"Lemme see!" Mr. Garibaldi says excitedly. He stares at the photos, exclaiming, *"Ah, ché bella!"*

"We do look dope together, right?" Dorinda says proudly.

"Ay, *Madonna*! I forgot the clams oreganato!" Mr. Garibaldi cries, then runs back to the kitchen to get his Italian creation out of the oven.

"Daddy should have his own cooking show," Galleria says, looking up from her notebook for a second.

"I saw you yesterday with Eddie Lizard," Chanel whispers in my ear. "Aqua has her first crush!"

"I do not," I whisper back. I cannot believe she is saying this with Galleria sitting right over there on the sofa! *"You* have a crush on him."

"I do not!" Chanel says, her brown eyes getting bigger than Ring Dings. "Well, maybe for a second—but then I remembered, I'm saving myself for Krusher!"

Angie snickers, and I cut my eyes at her. Krusher is Chanel's favorite singer—but not ours.

Meanwhile, Ms. Dorothea drops a pan, and it makes a loud noise, almost scaring us to death. We're all still jumpy after the weekend's events. Ms. Dorothea sticks her head out of the kitchen and snaps, "Galleria, please put the good glasses on the table like I asked you to. And get your nose out of that notebook!"

Galleria reluctantly obeys.

"It would be one thing if you were doing your homework, but I know you're writing a song," Ms. Dorothea continues, shooing their dog Toto into the kitchen to eat his dinner from his bowl. "My goodness, you probably have enough songs to give to the Goodwill by now!"

Oooh, I know *that* hurt! I never heard Ms. Dorothea fussing at Galleria before about writing songs. I guess Galleria must have done *something* to upset her mom, and I'm sure we're gonna hear about it later tonight, when we go into the chat room on the Internet for our Cheetah Girls Council meeting.

"Done, diddly, done, Mom," Galleria says, jumping up and plopping her Kitty Kat notebook on the chair. "Someone find me the key to the doghouse, pleez!"

"Well, one more phone call from that amphibian boy, and you'll be living in a snake pit!" Ms. Dorothea hisses. "Back in my day, a boy called the house once a day to keep the doctor away—not every hour, like he's on the admitting team in ER!"

We gather from the tone in Ms. Dorothea's voice that Eddie Lizard must be wearing out his welcome with Ma Bell—at least at the Garibaldi residence! Galleria clams up, and keeps rubbing one of the glasses with a napkin, like she's removing an invisible spot.

"That's enough, Galleria!" Ms. Dorothea snaps. "You'd think you were rubbing Aladdin's lamp to make three wishes!"

"The glasses are beautiful," Dorinda pipes up.

"Thank you—we got them at the Galleria," Ms. Dorothea says, then lets out a little smile.

"Oh? When did you go to the Galleria?" I ask, surprised. I know Ms. Dorothea wanted to come down to Houston for Thanksgiving, but had to stay and work on her winter collection for her store.

"Darling, I mean the Galleria in Milan."

"Oh," I say, surprised. "I didn't know they had a Galleria in Milan—um, Italy?" I know Bubbles was named after the Galleria Mall in Houston. Ms. Dorothea told us that the first time we met her.

"Oh, you didn't know, Aquanetta?" Mr. Garibaldi says, his eyes lighting up. "The *original* Galleria is in Milano—it's been there for centuries. The one in Houston is copied after that—the gigantic, glasslike roof, the marvelous cafes, *everything*. But they are both beautiful, of course!"

"We didn't even know that, and we're from Houston," Angie exclaims, impressed.

"Are you ready for a feast?" Mr. Garibaldi says, "because this is one you'll never forget."

"Yes, we are!"

Finally, Ms. Dorothea plops herself down at the head of the dining room table, and massages her temples like she has a headache. "What a day I had. Queen Latifah's stylist came in, and worked my store over like a rattlesnake in sand! I mean, she left not one grain unturned. I have nothing left to sell but a few boas!"

"Word?" Dorinda responds, amused. She majors in fashion design at school, so she's very into it, and laps up everything Ms. Dorothea says like a cat with a bowl of condensed milk.

Mr. Garibaldi sets all the food on the table, and we start salivating. Whatever he calls the dish he's made, it looks dee-licious.

"Lobster fra diavolo, just like my mother used to make for us on Sundays," Mr. Garibaldi says proudly. "Believe me, this recipe has been in the Garibaldi family long before that other Garibaldi freed Rome!"

"What other Garibaldi?" Angie asks, curious.

"In Italy, he's like our Martin Luther King. You know, a hero who fought for the people and led a revolution," Galleria explains proudly.

"Is that right?" Daddy asks, sucking up his pasta dish. I can't believe how much Daddy is eating—like a horse after winning the Kentucky Derby!

The phone rings, and Galleria jumps up to get it. "No, I'll get it," Ms. Dorothea says firmly, standing up—and almost touching the ceiling because she is so *tall*. "I'm warning you now, Galleria, if that Lizard boy is calling you again, then I'm calling Batman and having him thrown out of Gotham!"

"What's he calling for?" Dorinda asks, raising her eyebrows innocently. Bless her heart, I don't think Dorinda even knows exactly what's going on!

"Oh, he just wants to talk about a little something, something," Galleria says, without looking up from her plate.

"Yeah, well, it sounds like a whole lot of nothing, nothing, if you ask me!" Ms. Dorothea huffs as she picks up the phone.

Angie and I look at each other, and I know we're thinking the same thing: *Can you believe the telephone is cheetah, too?*

"Hello?" Ms. Dorothea says, in her sweet phone voice.

I look at Galleria, but she's trying to act like she doesn't care who's on the phone.

"Oh, hello, Mr. Mouse Almighty! Pardon me for saying this, but fancy hearing from you at dinnertime on a Sunday night!"

I almost choke on the strand of linguini I'm sucking into my mouth. Now all five of us look at each other, like, "She did not say Mouse

Almighty, the producer from Def Duck Records, did she!?!"

"Oh, we're just having some lobster fra diavolo, clams oreganato, and homemade gelato with chocolate cannolis for dessert—but nothing special, just another Sunday dinner."

Ms. Dorothea walks back to the dinner table with the phone. "Oh, heavens, no. I couldn't cook an egg with a timer. No, my husband gets all the credit. Perhaps we can tempt you. . . . No? Okay, but I insist you come another time. Yes, yes, I understand. It must be difficult. Yes, the girls will be delighted. I'll check with their schedule and get back to you. Hmm. Hmm. Good-bye."

We stare at Ms. Dorothea like she has swallowed the fortune cookie with the fortune still inside.

"Was that *the* Mouse?" Galleria asks, like she's holding her breath.

"Yes, Mouse is definitely in the house," Ms. Dorothea says slowly, picking up her fork to resume eating her dinner.

"Where is he?" Galleria asks, like she's bursting.

"He's in the park, feeding pigeons," Ms. Dorothea says, smirking. "Where do you think he is—in the studio, where we have to go see him!"

"Omigod!" I say, letting out a big sigh.

"I must say, these music biz people are strange birds," Ms. Dorothea says, shaking her head. "He says he's been up all night finishing Kahlua's album, but in the next breath he says he's ready to get the Cheetah Girls into the studio. I don't think he knew what day of the week it was, or what time."

"Well, *we* know what time it is!" Galleria shrieks, beside herself—and believe me, she's not alone! Angie and I can barely sit still in our chairs! If our daddy wasn't here, we would get up and start "whoopin' and hollerin'." 'Cuz believe me, this news is something to get excited about. *Hee-haw!*

"So, when are you girls available to go into the studio?" Ms. Dorothea asks, but she already knows the answer.

"Tomorrow at sunrise!" Galleria shouts out.

"Well, we have a little matter that I didn't want to discuss with Mouse," Ms. Dorothea says, looking right at Chanel. "There is no need for Mouse Almighty to know about Chanel's little ballet escapade."

Chanel turns five shades of red, and begins to protest. "But, *Madrina*—"

"No buts, Chanel—especially after you landed on yours during that audition!" Ms. Dorothea continues, like a locomotive couldn't stop her if it tried. "We're going to wait until Chanel can walk without crutches, which shouldn't be more than another week."

"I can walk without them *now*! *Te juro*—I swear! I only use them because *Mamí* makes me!" Chanel's big brown eyes are pleading like a puppy dog's.

"Well, I'm going to call Mouse back tomorrow, and make an appointment for next week. That will give you all time to practice together, and for Chanel to get her balance back. Is that a deal?"

"A wheela-deala!" Galleria says.

"*Ma che fortuna!* Look at the luck that Sunday dinner together brought you," exclaims Mr. Garibaldi. He's waving his fork and knife in both hands, like a kid who just got a big, shiny, red Mack truck for his birthday!

"You are right, Mr. Garibaldi—this is a feast we'll *never* forget!" I say. I'm so grateful for everything—for being in the Cheetah Girls, for helping Daddy come back to his senses, and for living in New York City—even though we miss Ma terribly.

"At long last, we're in the house with Mouse!" Galleria says, reaching over to hug her mother. "And that definitely means mo' betta chedda for the Cheetah Girls!"

Do' Re Mi on the Q.T.

This is Galleria and this is Chanel
We are coming to you live
From Cheetah Girls Central
Where we process the data that matters
And even mad chatter
But today we're here to tell you
About our friend, Do' Re Mi
(That's Miss Dorinda to you)
Kats and Kittys, the drama
Has gotten so radikkio
Just when we thought we knew our crew
Bam! The scandal was told!

There's a new girl in town
That's Miss Dorinda to you,
She bounced into our lives
But now she's part of our crew

Do' Re Mi on the Q.T.
Do' Re Mi on the D.D.L.

(That ain't swell)
Do' Re Mi on the Q.T.
Do' Re Mi on the D.D.L.
(Why won't you tell?)

Dorinda's got a secret
And it's cutting off her flow
(Is that right, girlita*?)*
According to our sources,
She thought we didn't know
(Kats and Kittys, you'd better take notes)
Today for the first time (the very first time)
Do' Re Mi found out she's not alone
(What are you saying?)
She found out she got a sister
And it's making her moan and groan!

There's a new girl in town
That's Miss Dorinda to you,
She bounced into our lives
But now she's part of our crew

Do' Re Mi on the Q.T.
Do' Re Mi on the D.D.L.
(That ain't swell)
Do' Re Mi on the Q.T.

Do' Re Mi on the D.D.L.
(Why won't you tell?)
But we peeped you!
And now we beeped you!
So what you know about that, huh?

Let's tell Miss Dorinda
That she's got all the flavor
And when she keeps things to herself
It's Do' Re Mi that we savor
Don't turn quiet on us
Like you got nothing to say
We found out you got a sister
So why can't she come out and play?

Do' Re Mi on the Q.T.
Do' Re Mi on the D.D.L.
(That ain't swell)
Do' Re Mi on the Q.T.
Do' Re Mi on the D.D.L.
(Why won't you tell, tell, tell!)
We said Do' Re Mi's on the Q.T.
(That's the sneak tip)
Do' Re Mi on the D.D.L.
(That's the down, down low)
Do' Re Mi on the Q.T.

Do' Re Mi on the D.D.L.

Do' Re Mi on the Q.T.
Who you trying to be?
Do' Re Mi on the D.D.L.
That's right, you know that's fowl
like a nearsighted owl
Do' Re Mi on the Q.T.
Why you got secrets
that make us growl?
Do' Re Mi on the D.D.L.
(Is that really true her sister is—Ahhhh!
Yes, mamacita . . . *)*

(Fade with growl sounds)

The Cheetah Girls Glossary

Bugaboo: Country hick. Pain in the neck. A boy who is kinda annoying.

Cigarette-leg pants: Fitted pants that taper down the bottom to a skinny leg. Very popular in the 1950s with poodle-carrying divas.

Crawling with crickets: Upset. Jumpy.

D.D.L.: On the down, down low. For example: You told Rerun that you couldn't go to the movies with him because you had homework to do, but then you go to the mall with your posse, and see him hanging with his. You run into the girls' room, and stay on the D.D.L. until the coast is clear.

Disco diva: Someone who reigned during the disco music period in the 1970s. Famous disco divas include Grace Jones, Donna Summer, and Gloria Gaynor, who defined the disco period with her anthem, "I Will Survive."

Fib-ulous tale: Something that only happened in your imagination.

Green-eyed monster: Jealousy. Envy. Example: "Dalissa was mackin' my new outfit so hard, I could tell she got bitten by the green-eyed monster."

Horse and pony show: Showing off. Drawing attention. Example: "At Brittany's birthday party, this rhythmnless boy and girl were in the middle of the dance floor, putting on a horse and pony show!"

Imbibe: Fancy way of saying drinking, or sipping liquid refreshments.

Inconspicuous: Out of sight. Hard to notice. For example, "Why don't you sit in the corner and try to be inconspicuous for a change and some coins."

Intervene: To get in the mix; cut in. Example: "Daddy is not feeling my report card, so maybe I'd better intervene on my behalf, and tell him I'll try harder next term."

Mackin': Checking something—or someone—over to the max.

Mo' betta chedda: More juice. More "ops." More caviar for the crackers!

Overstand: When you can see things like they really are—without a crystal ball.

Pecan nut: Someone who is fruitier than Froot

Loops, and definitely doesn't have an elevator that goes all the way to the penthouse! In other words, a little cuckoo!

Q.T.: On the hush-hush, sneak-sneaky, or the quick tip.

Salutation: Greeting. Example: "Hey, Dim Sum, where's the yum-yum?"

Shabby: Terrible. Tacky. Shameless. Example: "Her outfit is so shabby."

Sound bytes: Tasty, quick riffs you do when you're giving radio or television interviews, and wanna sound like you're at the top of your game.

Talisman charm: A symbolic item used in spells or for good luck. Can be worn around the neck, carried in a pouch, or placed on a worship altar.

Withholding information: Not exactly a fiberoni or white lie; more like keeping a secret.

ABOUT THE AUTHOR

Deborah Gregory earned her growl power as a diva-about-town contributing writer for ESSENCE, VIBE, and MORE magazines. She has showed her spots on several talk shows, including OPRAH, RICKI LAKE, and MAURY POVICH. She lives in New York City with her pooch, Cappuccino, who is featured as the Cheetah Girls' mascot, Toto.

 JUMP AT THE SUN

Hey, Girlfriend!

Would you like to be a member of our club?

Just for me! by PRO-LINE

VIP CLUB

Black History
Profiles
Internet Safety
VIP Parties

Join Today!

Become a Just for Me VIP Member and get the official club membership kit today!
The membership kit includes a Just for Me VIP Club: Membership Card, Newsletter, Do Not Disturb Door Hanger, Passport to Fun, Scrungies, Bookmark, Coupons, ID Fingerprint Card, and Membership Flyer. In addition, you will receive a birthday card, a birthday surprise, and bimonthly newsletters.

Official Enrollment Form: Make sure you fill this form out completely. Print clearly. We cannot be responsible for lost, late, misdirected, or illegible mail. Enclose $9.95 plus one Just for Me proof of purchase (front panel), for membership in the JFM VIP Club, or $19.95 with no proof of purchase. Make check or money order (no cash) payable to: Just for Me VIP Club c/o Pro-Line Corp., P.O. Box 222057, Dallas, Texas 75222-9831

Name: _____ Date of Birth: _____

Address: _____

City: _____ State: _____ ZIP: _____

Day Phone: _____ Evening Phone: _____

Parent signature: _____

ail membership forms to: Pro-Line Corporation   Attn: JFM VIP Club Membership   P.O. Box 222057   Dallas, TX 75222-9831

The Pro-Line Company is not affiliated with The Walt Disney Company